THE
ROVING
PARTY

THE
ROVING
PARTY

ROHAN WILSON

First published in 2011 by Allen & Unwin
Sydney, Melbourne, Auckland, London

Published by
Soho Press, Inc.
853 Broadway
New York, NY 10003

Library of Congress Cataloging-in-Publication Data

Wilson, Rohan.
The roving party / Rohan Wilson.
p cm.
ISBN 978-1-61695-311-9
eISBN 978-1-61695-312-6
1. Aboriginal Tasmanians—Ethnic identity—Fiction.
2. AboriginalTasmanians—Treatment—Fiction. I. Title.
PR9619.3.W5845R68 2014
823'.914—dc23   2013025993

Typeset in 13.5/19.5 pt Spectrum by Post Pre-press Group, Brisbane, Australia

Printed in the United States of America

10 9 8 7 6 5 4 3 2 1

Rohan Wilson lived a long, mostly lonely, life until a lucky turn of events led him to take up a teaching position in Japan where he met his wife. They have a son who loves books, as all children should. They live in Launceston but don't know why. Rohan holds degrees and diplomas from the universities of Tasmania, Southern Queensland and Melbourne. This is his first book. He can be found on Twitter: @rohan_wilson.

THEY WHISTLED FOR BLACK BILL THROUGH the foredawn and called his old clan name behind it, a name he had no good use for. He sat upright on the bed and looked about. The fire in the hearth was dead and the hut utterly without light. He doubled the blanket over his woman, covering the small mound of her belly. He pulled on his hat, his boots, all the while listening to those distant souls whistling and calling as if he was some game dog meant for the hunt. Then he swung the bark doorflap outwards and stood in its hollow watching the huge columned gums slowly gain distinction as the sun flared. In the thin hews of light the air was damp and misted and he was staring a good few moments before he noticed them. First the wormy dogs half hidden in the fog bands. Then ranged out in the steaming scrub reefs something arrived as if from an ether dream. Black Bill clenched his teeth. It was a hunting party of Plindermairhemener men.

They watched him across the mists, gripping clusters of spears like long slender needles. Kangaroo mantles hung loosely off their frames to hide the costume pieces beneath, trousers old and torn and black with the blood of game they had taken and looted cotton shirts gone to rags. One of their number was got up in an infantryman's crosswebbing and another was fitted out in a fine worsted coat as if dressed for dinner. Their breath bled in the cold. Not a cast of relics come out of the grasslands where their forebears had walked but men remade in ways peculiar to this new world. As he watched those figures from the doorway the Vandemonian felt for the knife he kept rigged between his shoulderblades.

Foremost among that singular horde was Manalargena who carried across his shoulder a waddy shaped from blackwood and stained with the filth of war. He twisted the tool as he led his party from the scrub flanked by a dog pack, the bark shattering beneath his feet. Manalargena was vain, had always been, and his wife had ochred his hair into long ringlets as precise as woven rope. Indeed all the men wore their hair in this fashion sculpted by the womenfolk but only the headman walked across that ground like a fellow enamoured of the sound of his own tread. mina bungercarner. nina bungercarner. mina tunapri nina. nina tunapri mina. He gazed into Bill's face as he spoke.

narapa. Black Bill lowered his knife.

The clansmen arranged themselves on the bare earth beside Bill's humpy and they gestured with open palms for him to sit also. They were freshly painted for war and when Manalargena offered him a muttonfish shell filled with grease and ochre the Vandemonian accepted it, removed his hat and dabbed the paint over his head. Bill wore his hair cut tightly short like the white men of the district but the clansmen watched him with solemn regard and if their opinion of it was scornful they gave no sign. The headman again addressed Bill and this time he did so partly in English by way of showing him his place. For the Vandemonian was as good as white.

Tummer-ti, he said. You come we need you. tunapri mina kani?

Black Bill studied his deeply creased face.

You come fight, the headman said.

Eh?

Fight with us.

Where? carnermema lettenener?

tromemanner.

Bill looked around at those grimly visaged men of war; each and every one met his eyes and he saw among their faces the bold expectations held for him.

You strong man you fight, the headman said. Come with us.

Black Bill was silent. He scratched at the old ritual scars on his chest. He called to his woman to leave her bed and when no reply came he called again, his words oddly deadened by the mist between the trees. Soon she showed in the doorway bundled in a blanket and Bill asked for the meat to be brought out.

tawattya, she said to the clansmen, but they looked away from her and shook their heads. Her hair, long for a black woman, seemed to upset them.

Her name what?

Bill faced the headman. Katherine.

Katarin, the headman said to her. You good woman. You bring food, Katarin. Bring tea. Good woman. We talk.

She stared at him. Then she vanished into the hut.

Manalargena smiled and waited until she returned with a cold joint of kangaroo. The clansmen ate freely and passed the billycan of tea around every mouth. Over the smack of lips the headman praised Bill for the fine wife he had taken, her obedience, her silence, and on a whim he stood and strutted in mockery of his own proud wife and raised their laughter with his portrayal of her arrogant bearing. The beard on his chin was matted, and the lank twists as red as a rooster's wattle jiggled while he walked about. Dark hands flapped at his sides and his nose turned high. The men of his party laughed but Bill watched and kept his tongue still.

Once more the headman sat among the men of his clan and reached for the billycan. He drank, wiped his mouth and looked towards Bill. In the doorway Katherine held her rounded belly. The headman waved a crooked finger at her.

She carry what?

I dont know, said Bill.

The headman studied her a moment and rubbed his plagued

left arm. It was a mass of scars where he'd tried to bleed the demon out in his youth.

Boy, he said. Strong boy. I know this.

The cold sun in the trees as it loomed over the hills picked out Manalargena's features, the folds of his face, the crosshatching rent in the flesh of his evil arm. Here was a man who might part the very weft of the world by his own words. A man sung up and down the island. The whites wanted him for hanging and several locals had stood their own private funds against the receipt of his head for campaigns conducted upon them by his clan. But Black Bill looked away from him.

The headman said, A boy. My demon tell me.

There was another elder among the party, an old man of skin and sinew, who summoned their eyes to himself by beating his waddy on his palm. He was called Taralta and his face was scarred and churlish. He alone in that clan knew the law and its application and he talked quietly into the hush his tapping had created. He spoke long against the whites and decried their contempt for peace with ancient turns of phrase Bill could not comprehend, metaphors that had lost sense for all but a few wizened lawkeepers. He called the whites the cawing of the crow for morning. An inundation driving his kind into the heights of the mountains, the peaks of the trees. He adduced a great litany of evils befouling his clan and on each point he drew attention to the culpability of the whites and the flagrant disregard they displayed for any notion of justice. He said that if you forgave the devil for eating your food, he would soon eat your children. Black Bill listened to the case put forth and when Taralta was finished he raised his eyes to the lawman's face.

I am obliged to Batman, he said, and no other.

Taralta frowned upon mention of that name. One or two of the seated clansmen, those who had something of the English language, saw through Bill's meaning and they rendered it for the lawman. They stared at the Vandemonian and waited for Manalargena to speak. But the headman was rubbing his bedevilled arm as new spasms appeared upon his shoulder, rippling and flexing beneath the skin. He closed his eyes and seemed intent on hearing whatever counsel it might whisper in whatever sordid tongue it used.

bungana Batman, the headman said with his eyes yet closed and his mouth turning ugly. Why you follow him?

The Vandemonian stood up. I got no more to say on the matter.

When he moved, the men of the hunting company also moved, pushing themselves up by their spears as the game dogs wheeled about, their eyes aflame in the dawn light. Manalargena climbed to his feet and slung his waddy across his shoulder.

Come fight, he said.

No.

I say this. Knife is sharpen on stone. You come now. We find your stone.

No.

Grey light curled above the gums. If there was more of a world beyond that small clearing and the few souls standing there, Bill knew nothing of it in those moments when the headman held him fixed in a glare. But he would not be moved.

My father, said Manalargena, he tell me many thing. He like to speak. And I like to listen. Now you hear me, Tummer-ti. You listen. As he spoke the headman moved his hand as if he was conjuring.

There was two brother you see. They live near a river them brother. They catch plenty crayfish in river. It was big river very big. They got long legs them brother they walk out that river and catch them crayfish. Under the rock. Then one brother he make the fire. Another brother he sing the song. Then they eat them crayfish you see. They sing and they eat. Always this way. They pass many happy day.

I remember it, said Bill. I heard it before.

You hear me, Tummer-ti. You listen.

Bill looked around at the others. A dour mob. I aint concerned with yer stories, he said.

But the headman went on. Hunter come to the river. He is hungry hunter you see. He want crayfish. He see them brother eating crayfish, singing song. He want crayfish too. He bring up spear. Here the headman made as if to raise something. He bring up that spear and he call out: I hungry, you give me

7

that crayfish. He hold that spear and he call out. But them brother they scared you see. They scared and they run. They run and they change. They change to wallaby and they jump. Now they jump and jump and the hunter he follow them.

So hunter he change too. He run and he change to that wallaby and he jump. Now three wallaby jump near river. They eat grass. They forget the crayfish. They eat grass and they drink water and they forget crayfish. Three wallaby near the river. Very big river.

Black Bill looked at him. They was snakes was how I heard it told.

Snake?

Aye. Snakes.

powrana?

powrana. Bill made a slithering motion with his hand.

No no no. Wallaby. You listen, Tummer-ti. You Panninher man not Plindermairhemener. You listen my story. Three wallaby near the river you see. Not two and one but three. Them brother lost, you understand. They see plenty wallaby. But no see brother. Three wallaby near river eat the grass and drink the water but they forget. Who is brother. Who is hunter. They forget this thing. Now three wallaby. No one sing. Them all lost. All same you see.

Bill looked the headman long in the eyes. That makes no sense, he said.

You no hear. Hear nothing. Manalargena tapped at his

temple. A wind was freshly risen in the gums and it dispersed the scrags of mist and shifted the headman's shirt.

I dont want no part of it, said Bill. You do what you think is right. Do what you have to. But I cant help.

The headman snorted. He glanced around at his warriors. They leaned on their long spears, puffs of vapour blowing from their nostrils as they stood in the cold, indifferent to the Vandemonian's refusal. But the headman rubbed his arm slowly as he looked Black Bill over one last time, then without a word he turned and led his clan off into the scrub, the slap of their feet sounding on the earth as they went. Bill waited as those figures melded once more into the bush and waited even after they'd gone, staring into the void, left with only his thoughts.

Inside the humpy he filled a tin bowl from the river bucket and unwrapped the soap cake from its leather. He lathered his hair and rinsed away the clay and possum grease smeared over it, the water running bloodcoloured off his forehead. He washed and rinsed once more. The collar of his shirt hung sodden and redstained about his neck as he ladled the water across his scalp and Katherine, huddled in her blankets, loaded the fire with wood and watched him.

When he was done, when he'd emptied the water outside, he went to the corner of the humpy and retrieved the old brown bessie kept beside their bed. It was a decent piece for which he'd bartered his pair of seasoned game dogs. He checked the mechanism, loaded it and propped the gun beside the door. Then he lowered himself into the chair and sat staring at the weapon. The roving party would be striking out after the Plindermairhemener in a week. Batman had agreed to cut him in on the bounty. Him and the Dharugs. Without their bushcraft the party had no hope of success.

Katherine eyed the gun.

You see them again you'll be needin it, he said.

But Bill knew the gun was only for show. If Manalargena means harm then harm shall follow.

THEY WOULD BE NINE. AS THE dray crawled over the hill it loomed long and blackshaped before the shallow sun, four prisoners hunched and jostling on the flatbed. On the verandah the company of native men passed a pipe among themselves and watched the dray clatter ever closer. Black Bill was among them, on his head a widebrimmed stockman's hat pushed in at the crown. He pulled his turn on the pipe and gave it along to Pigeon as the cart inched down the mud track onto Kingston farm. With the Vandemonian, John Batman and his manservant Gould, the Dharug men Crook and Pigeon newly come from the Parramatta, and now the lags on the flatbed, there would be nine all told for the roving party.

The dray drew up beside the farmhouse, a cockeyed hut hewn from the stuff of the scrub, and the shackled men on the bed looked it over as if it was pestilent. Walled with rounds of gumtree, roofed with bark shingles and bleeding smoke from a stone chimney, its harsh angles were entirely at odds with the fields and hills behind it. A pair of soldiers stepped off the bench seat and they trained their firearms upon the prisoners.

Come off there, you bastards, said the senior man, the overseer.

The fettered men, clanging like dulled cowbells, shuffled across the planks of the bed and clambered to the ground. With the stock of his firearm the overseer formed them into a line beside the cart.

Now pay attention to me, he said. Pay it good. Or I will carve my name into the first dogfucker what doesnt. He brandished his weapon before them, pushing aside his red coat, long since faded to a womanly pink, elbows mended with hide.

You hold that line and keep yer damn eyes on that mud there. You ponder on that mud cause damn my livin soul if you lot aint more useless than a hatful of it. I'm talkin to you, you old pisser. Bloody look at me when I talk.

They are a mongrel lot.

Black Bill looked around. William Gould had come up from the back paddocks and was addressing Bill as he stood watching. In his castoffs Gould made barely a better sight than the prisoners but he drew his face into a frown at the state of the new men as his eyes swept over them. Rag and bone and bugger-all else, he said.

Seems that way, said Bill.

One of the four prisoners was a roundshouldered old cur and this fellow fixed the overseer with a malicious stare.

Eyes down, you dog, eyes down. Dont you bloody look at me! The overseer was signalling with two fingers for the prisoner to lower his gaze. Keep your damn eyes off me, he said.

The prisoner dropped his head but his disdain remained and the rest of the shabby lot said not a word as the junior private shifted along to unchain their basils and toss them ringing onto the flatbed. Now freed, the men rubbed their abraded ankles, waiting for whatever came next.

Then Gould called out, Here he comes.

They all turned as John Batman appeared. He stood in the shadow thrown by the house. In his hands was a dead lamb, its head hacked off. When he walked forward into the pale sunlight he was as bloody as a surgeon and he held the carcass out before him. Its fleece was red and blood trailed over the mud behind him.

Bickle. I supposed they'd send you, he said, his breath steaming in the cold. He had a voice serrated by the overuse of his pipe and a fondness for rum taken straight. How was the roads?

The overseer wore a smile that was forced upon him. No trouble, Mr. Batman. No trouble at all.

For your wife, said Batman.

Bickle took the tiny headless thing. She'll be most pleased she will.

Batman met him with a fierce eye. You got that money yet?

Now I told you about that, said Bickle and laughed. A short tight cough. It wasnt no fairly drawn hand.

Batman moved closer. So you're callin me a swindler?

I'm callin you a swindler. A chiseller. A bilker. You choose whichever suits you best. Pleased with himself, the overseer looked around at his mate and at the black men arranged upon Batman's verandah.

There was a little swell about Batman's throat where he swallowed the word he'd almost used. Remember where you are, he said.

All I know is you turned a knave when it was needed. And knaves dont come up too often.

Well it come up. Now you owe me.

I owe you? Christ. Let a man be, would you. That canny luck of yours will show next time we front up to the table. By God it will. You might just have your money then.

Batman nodded, a slow and measured rocking of the head, but he showed no satisfaction. The horse huffed and shied in her harness. Behind the farmhouse the gum trees lashed in the winds. Batman walked before the line of men who stood with their heads bowed, shivering in their rough hessians. You have been told no doubt what I mean to see through, he said. What that means for youse fellows is this: if you've no stomach for killin, say so now.

The four men looked about but each kept quiet.

Then you are with me, he said. Batman's shirt and coat sleeves were rolled back showing his forearms pasted with a slick of lamb's blood. He wiped his arms with a rag, returned it to his pocket and unfurled his sleeves. Staring at the men, he continued: Now I've as much regard for peace as anyone but I've been given a contract by the Governor and I intend to collect on it.

The men shifted nervously.

How many ayou had seen a black before today? He indicated with a nod of his head the two men of the Parramatta where they leaned their long bodies against the uprights of his verandah. The new men seemed unsure of what he expected. He came around to where he might better catch their eyes or look down into their grubby weathered faces. You boy?

No sir.

No?

No sir, not a one.

Well take a look. Go on. They're tamed.

The boy raised his eyes, as did the rest, to study the three black men, and in turn they regarded the prisoners across that open space of rutted grass and mud which served as a turning circle for carts. The black men were alike in bearing and build, tall and well shaped for bush life, properly clothed but for their bare feet. Pigeon kept himself shaved and tended and made a fine figure in his calico jacket but his mate, John Crook, wore on his head a red wool cap marred with filth and holes. It was Crook who leaned forward and addressed the new men in his own language, his hand waving in anger.

Thinks it's white dont it, said the old cur. Dressed up like that.

A cold silence followed. Pigeon came down off the verandah and stepped forward. For a moment he put out his hand
to the men as any gentleman might but withdrew it when they
plainly ignored him. Maybe they did not know what to make
of him, a free man in the employ of Batman, or perhaps they
saw in him something of their own failings. Only the boy put
out his hand for Pigeon.

Good evenin, said Pigeon.

They shook hands.

Here John Batman interrupted the niceties. He addressed
the prisoners. These fellows are of a different turn, he said, and
as he motioned towards the black men the folds of his greatcoat flapped like canvas sails. They've had something of the
wildness beaten out of them. Something, I say; not everything.
Now the sort you shall encounter in the scrub hereabouts will
not shake yer hand. My word. They are a people . . .

He looked along the row of faces all fixed upon him and the
wind blew as cold as river water funnelled through the foothills below the white cotton crown of Ben Lomond, and it set
his eyes glistening. Here was a man speaking in deep passion,
fullhearted, enjoining them to rise up in common cause. The
lags watched him, trying to still their chattering teeth.

A people who havent the smallest inclination towards layin
down for us.

From a pocket of his coat Batman produced a quart flask of
Indian rum that ran thickly up the glass then resettled. He pulled

the stopper as he repeated, Not the smallest, and threw back a swallow. The Governor is payin us to instil a lesson in the obtuse skulls of these dark skins. But I tell you this right now. It may be the blacks what do the instilling. It may be them affixing our bodies to the trees as you would the common criminal of old. I will offer no indemnity against that outcome. None whatsoever.

Shoals of cloud glowed blood red on the horizon and the sun cast Batman tall and intense. The wind crashed in the blue gums along the hills and squalled down the valley. But the four men by the dray studied the ground in silence. From another pocket Batman produced a cake of negro head. He approached the assigned men and placed it in the palm of a fellow who grinned through his black beard and fixed Batman with his one good eye.

You are a top sort, you are, he said to Batman. Look here, lads, we have some chew for ourselfs. He divided the cake four even ways. They rubbed loose the fibres and dipped a wad into the folds of their cheeks.

As they chewed Batman spoke. There is among them a chief. A warrior. Some say witch. He is called Manalargena. If we dont kill this man we all need a floggin, I tell you. Mark him by his beard which he keeps dressed with ruddle. You must bring him down before all others.

The men spat strings of juice on the ground, nodded their heads and mopped their chins, their eyes always upon Batman.

. . .

Sergeant Bickle pointed at a line on the printed warrant. Make your mark here if you would, he said. It was a crumpled certificate he'd pulled from inside his coat and flattened out upon the bench of the horsecart. Batman read the thing over with narrowed eyes then carried the paper inside his house to sign his name to it. In that time Bickle put the new men to unloading from the dray sacks marked flour, tea, sugar and tobacco. In the low sun their shadows grew long and spidered, a procession of fairytale horrors shifting over the turf and all the while he goaded them with threats of a skinning at the end of his whip.

Look here, Black Bill said to Batman as he returned with the warrant. They dont have shoes.

Batman studied the bare feet slopping through the mud as they worked to unload. He raised his hat, smoothed back his hair and then resettled the hat neatly on his crown. He looked around at the overseer.

Sergeant Bickle, where are their shoes?

Dont recall I saw no shoes on the requisition.

You what?

I dont recall I—

What use are the bastards without shoes?

I done what I was ordered. Address your request to the Police Magistrate and he'll dispatch em.

Batman shook his head. That no-account wants a ball sendin through his bloody brains.

Seems your crows dont need shoes. Bickle raised his gun

at the Parramatta blacks and clicked his tongue. They glared at the soldier where he stood mocking them, their hands tight around the uprights and their jaws firmly set. A month ago the Dharug men had been walking the browned grasslands of New South Wales, but now their feet sank inch deep in the miserable damp of Van Diemen's Land. They'd trod the August snow slurries and the mud and river marshes and felt the thorns of the pines through their soles and they would not be shod by anyone.

Christ look at the boots on that bastard, said Bickle as he lowered his firearm. Black Bill had on a pair of boots cut in the fashion of a horseman and shined up fresh. The stitching was waxed and white against the boots and the leather had been polished with a lump of glass, much in the manner of saddle skirting, to give it a high gloss.

He's stolen them from somebody, said Bickle.

John Batman looked him straight in the face. I tell you what. You get them off his feet and you can keep em.

The overseer worked a spit cud around his mouth while he took stock of Black Bill from hat to heels, his hostile eyes betraying his opinion of what he saw there.

You get them off his feet and I'll call it quits on that money. Call it square.

Bickle nodded slackly, spat on the dirt.

Go and show him some sport. He aint much.

What is he? Six foot?

Sixish. But he's as untrained as the dog in the street.

That's as may be.

A man of your history ought not to worry. I've seen you put down worse than him.

Bickle never took his eyes off the black man where he was stationed upon the verandah. Quits, you say?

My word on it.

Aye. Well then.

He removed his cap and shrugged off his regimental coat before he approached the farmhouse where the Vandemonian was waiting. Bickle's rotten boots squelched over the ground; he dropped his cap on the mud and with a small motion of the fingers called Bill down.

Black Bill was a big fellow. He dipped his head under the crossbeam as he stepped off the decking, his dark face shadowed beneath his hat brim. When he moved, the musculature beneath the gleam of his skin drew taut, the cords of his forearms like pulleys. He seemed ignorant or perhaps contemptuous of the sergeant's intent for he never removed his hat. He waited there before the farmhouse a picture of calm. The assignees had caught on to the happenings Batman had stirred up and they dropped their loads, gathering near the dray to better see what might follow.

The overseer called out. Come ere now, he said, and givem up. He raised his naked fists like some village pugilist calling men to take the ring for a shilling.

20

Bill maintained his ground, raising one open hand. Watch yourself, was all he said.

But the overseer closed that distance by skipping his feet to hold his stance correct. He lashed out with a right. Bill was up to the task. He moved his head and shuffled back and when the overseer came again faster he struck out with his fist. The strike sat the soldier on his hindquarters. He was up smartly but Bill was over him and snapped him straight to the face hard. The overseer staggered under the blow. He stepped back and drew a hand across his face. Blood messing the front of his filthy undershirt. Blood in his teeth like a fiend on the kill.

You're done for fucker, he said. From inside some disguised pocket of his coat he retrieved a little highland dirk and circled Bill with the blade outheld, bloody strings swinging from his chin. You miserable nigger, he said.

The overseer feinted with the dirk and Bill pulled away. As he lunged again, Bill swayed back sinuously but the blade opened a gash in his shirt. He removed his hat and tossed it aside and his eyes were dark as coals. He assessed the overseer where he held position, dirk gripped for another pass. Warm blood spilled down the inside of his shirt. He said nothing. Instead he came forward with renewed precision, with a cold certainty about his every movement.

The overseer watched him. Then he lunged, the blade passing near Bill's chest and slicing back again but the Vandemonian timed his swing and caught the overseer across the chin with a punch that sent his head around brutally. He stumbled but held his feet. Already the swelling around his eye was growing blue and bulbous and he turned his head as if he was seeing his suroundings for the first time. Bill allowed him a moment to find what he could in the way of sense. The overseer looked around at the gathered men but no one spoke for a calloff. He spat out more blood and stepped closer.

This time he made no feints but moved straight into attack. Bill grappled his arms and they fell, each clutching the other, the knife blade flashing. The Vandemonian caught a handful of hair and yanked back the overseer's head, ramming his forehead into the soldier's face. Bickle was put out cold in that instant and Bill rolled off him. He stood up, retrieved his hat and checked the cut on his ribs. From where he lay the overseer raised one hand and let it fall again onto the mud and he moaned and gagged.

Black Bill came alongside him and John Batman also and together they raised him upright, those loosened eyes rolling about in their skull holes as he tottered to his feet. His lips and nose like broken fruit beneath his overgrowth of russet hair.

That's a goodun, Bill said to the overseer.

He raised his head. A goodun? he said.

Bill dipped his head towards the dirk.

Aye, said Bickle. She cuts fair. Good Scottish steel that. Bickle's bleeding mouth stumbled over his words. You cut?

Not much, said Bill. He touched his chest.

Those men who'd gathered in audience whispered between themselves and stared at the black man until John Batman waved them away.

He's flogged you like a rented mare.

The overseer took up his knife where it lay on the grass and cleaned the blade on his forearm. He spoke to Batman without looking up. He made his case. I see now I was in error.

Seems you still owe me though, dont it.

You bloody scoundrel. You'll have yer money.

With that Bickle was gone back to the dray, coat in hand and rank with blood, and his junior climbed aboard also and they departed.

The razor wind plying through the fields caused Bill to pinch up his eyes. In the far distance the sheep turned as if blown so by the winds and Bill sat a spell on the verandah watching the last of the sun. Every spring this wind bowled down from the hills, curling the trees over and setting the clouds skating out of the east. The clansfolk followed that salted breeze from the coast into the western hills where the snow dried before it and they harried the kangaroo herds of the lowland plains with their spears, their dogs. He held his cut chest and gazed up at the mountain. Their kind would soon have more than the wind for company.

Batman appeared, cocked one boot up on the decking, leaned on his knee. Well, he pulled a blade. As you said he would.

Bill looked up at him. He knows no better.

Sharp little bastard it was too.

In the quiet that followed they watched the dray haul away up the track with the wheel rims showering gobs of mud and the horse straining at the yoke.

mina carney he mengana knife, he said to Batman.

narapa, said Batman. mina tunapri.

DAWN CREPT UP LIKE A SICKLY pale child. William Gould walked over the frosted ground to the stables and went man to man, nudging the assignees awake with the toe of his boot. He dropped a pile of clothing on the ground and stood by as the assignees stripped out of their slops. They pulled on the pants and undershirts and workshirts. A turned and mended coat was among the pile and the boy had hold of it but he was shoved off by the blackbeard who wrenched the coat onto his own back. Over everything they hung rawhide tunics stitched from an assortment of skins that shared little accord of colour or shape, and bound their feet in the castoff slops for want of shoes, glancing about at each other but saying nary a word against it.

Outside in the sunshine Ben Lomond was a rise of crag and battlement white with silvered snow. The mountain's shadow jagged across the fields but where sunlight fell, the frost glittered salty white. The assignees squinted as they took stock of the squares of land girdled by chock and log fences: the mix of bigboned mutton ewes and Bengal-cross cattle meant for their beef, the little shepherd huts smoking serenely against the morning sky. Likely to their eyes the whole of Kingston farm was a swath of order hacked out of chaos, a stamp of authority hammered into Van Diemen's Land.

But when Bill surveyed that grant he saw the ancient constructions of the Plindermairhemener, the precisely burned plains carved over generations to advantage the hunter, the lands called up anew with every footfall. He found John Batman working at his shambles. A ewe laid open at the throat was raised up by her hocks by a block and tackle. Batman leaned against her as he peeled the woollen skin away with a finely bladed knife which he stropped occasionally on a belt hung from the cross frame. The pooled blood beneath the ewe was flecked with ants and strands of her viscera hung from the stomach cavity. Black Bill held the ewe's foreleg outwards as Batman sawed the shoulder, and as he bent the leg backwards against the joint the bones popped in the silence.

Said Batman: You seen them smokes?

I seen em.

The campfire smokes hung in the sky, long and white and bending in the winds, emanating from some deeply hidden quarter to the east of the mountain. Country known only by the clans that walked it.

How far you reckon?

Bill examined the luminous blue above the hills. Eight mile, he said. Ten.

They wont wait for us.

No, they wont.

The foreleg came away under Batman's knife and Bill moved it onto the butchering stand nearby. Batman towelled his arms clean. These reprobates will eat better than landed gentry by Christ.

No sooner had he spoken than the men in question came towards them from the stables, led by William Gould. They made a miserable sight dressed out in furs and barefoot but for the rags bound and tied at their ankles. Gould had in his arms a collection of fowling pieces which he gave out to the assignees and they turned those pieces in survey. They were weapons worn by the passing of a thousand hands and of that selection not one was fit for any purpose more than culling sick animals. The rust had been filed back along the barrels, the stocks nailed up where the weather had split the grain, and they'd been slung off kangaroo-skin lanyards barely tanned and lined still with fur.

John Batman looked along the rank. Your name?

Jimmy Gumm.

What?

Jimmy Gumm, sir.

You?

It's James Clarke, sir. Most calls me Horsehead, but.

And you, Maypole?

Howell Baxter, sir.

Welshman are you?

That I am, Mr. Batman.

You shot a man before, Maypole?

Not without call, Mr. Batman.

Well you have call now.

Baxter tapped his weapon. This here gun aint much good, he said.

That particular piece had been restraightened under the blunt side of an axe and was now given to firing along a lunatic trajectory. He made to hand the damaged firearm back but Batman only stared at him.

They'll make fine sport without a gun. Fine sport.

The assignee lowered his eyes and held the gun to his chest. Stood off aways was a boy of hardly gaoling age. He had his arms wrapped around himself against the cold and he scowled at the men and their business.

Do you know guns, lad?

I do.

The other men shook their heads. He dont know nothin of the sort, said Horsehead.

He has a knack for lyin, dont yer, said Gumm.

They all watched the boy, shivering in his outsized clothes, glaring back at those men, daring them to come at him.

Batman nodded his head and waved Gould over. He passed

a weapon to the boy. Either way you'll know it soon enough, he said.

A wooden balance and a pack of iron weights were taken from the store shed along with the sacks of flour, tea and sugar. William Gould put the men to measuring the flour into ten-pound portions. Sugar and tea were split between the men at sugar three ounces a day and tea a half-ounce. Once packed these rations would feed them for a week as they walked the back country, forty pounds or more hauled in kangaroo-skin bags. Gould held the balance while the men cut down the portions then took their weight against an iron counter, the little sacks being tied off with twine as they were finished. Batman stood by in his heavy greatcoat sipping rum from his flask and supervising the work as it progressed.

Do you have a name? Batman said to the boy.

Thomas.

Lad, you waste that flour and you go hungry.

The boy brushed what flour he could off his arms into the open mouths of the portion sacks. The tendons showed through the skin of his neck as he looked up. His hair would have been a fair sandy shade but for being matted with muck and it sat square razored across his forehead. He gave the gravest of nods and went on adding flour to one side of the scales.

Jimmy Gumm watched the boy also. He put down a sack of tea-leaves from which he was measuring, spat in his hands and rubbed them over. Be a good boy and hand me another, he said.

The boy paused in his work. I aint yer boy.

No. You was mine I'd beat three colours of snot from you.

The others laughed.

What are you laughing at? said the boy. They looked at him and by turns they bent their heads back to their portioning. Jimmy Gumm leaned over and removed from the pile beside Thomas a little knotted sack. As he moved away he cuffed the boy once around the ear, a decently weighted blow that rocked the boy backwards, before Gumm returned to filling the bags with tea-leaves. Sheep wailed far off, their lonely mewling matching the boy's low voice when he spoke. You wont touch me no more if you know what's good fer you, he said.

Wont I now.

No.

There was an eeriness about Gumm's eyes, one of which wandered loose of the other. I know what he done, he said. I know what Jock's Mal done to you. He done what he done to all the lads.

The boy kept his face down. The other men watched him scratch his forehead and leave a track of flour there.

He was puttin it around that lockup. Choice words they was too. Told to anyone who'd listen. Jock's Mal said to me, he said, Jim, I never even got a squeal out of the little devil.

The men laughed anew. The boy's face remained blank as he worked from the flour sack filling the smaller one at his feet.

He scooped up more and filled another sack, the drifts of powder rising about him as he worked.

You'd best be careful, boy. Elsewise you might get more of the same out there in the quiet of the wilds. A young buck like you. This time Gumm wasn't laughing.

The boy ceased what he was doing. In one action he picked up his heavyended fowling piece and flipped it about and took it by the barrel. Two white handprints were left upon the stock. He stepped towards Gumm, moving like a man at some trifling matter.

What's this? Gumm glared up at him. But even while the words were shapes in his mouth the boy was bringing the butt down across his skull. As he raised his arms the boy swung again, full and heaving, and Gumm cried out. No one made any movement towards them. Thomas struck again. Blood ran freely from Gumm's forehead. He scurried off across the bare earth on his hands and knees and the boy followed him. Whaling him over the back. Christ Jesus Christ Jesus, Gumm was saying.

A final blow then Gumm went limp. The boy held the piece ready but brought it down no more. John Batman pushed back his coat and ran his eyes over Gumm where he was laid out cold in the muck.

Turn him over so he dont choke at least, he said.

The boy rolled the fellow over and stood looking down on the battery he'd done as the life inched back into Gumm. He walked back to his bags with the eyes of the other men on his every step.

You save that for the blacks, said Batman. No bastard here wants to see it.

The boy never even glanced at him. He went once more about the packing and weighing of flour, tying off each sack as he went. He kept himself tightly drawn but those men saw the jitter in his fingers and heard his quick breaths.

. . .

The axe rang upon the fragrant hardwood and Katherine raised it once more and brought it down. The head bit deep and split the log evenways. She reached for one fallen half and sat the hunk again on the block where she cut that piece also into pieces, every sound of the axe coming back a second later off the mountain. She had a decent pile cut for Mrs. Batman's stove and wanted only a few more for the fireplace. The handle rasped in her palms as her upper hand slipped down the polished wood. The blade passed cleanly through the log and buried in the block beneath. She stood there in the new silence, her hands still on the handle, looking across the grazing land. In her belly the baby struggled and she put a hand there to contain it.

We'll be back in a week or so.

She turned around. Black Bill was standing with his hat in his hands, running the brim through his calloused fingers. She turned away and tugged the axe head loose of the block and brought the weight down upon a square of wood, the collision jarring her arms.

Mrs. Batman will put you up here at night. In one of the huts.

I go home.

She pulled up the axe as Bill stood by watching her minutely. Over the paddocks the shepherds were rousing their flocks for the pens. Otherwise there was just the scratching of Bill's hat in his fingers.

And what if nine aint enough to take him? said Bill. What then?

bungana Manalargena not hurt me.

Woman, he'll string yer limbs from the trees.

No. I go home.

Bill slowly exhaled. Think of the child.

She turned to face him. I think. Always. But you, you follow Batman.

He puts food in front of us. We are in his debt.

Dont eat his food.

Well, he said. I'm wasting breath here.

He replaced his hat and headed down the grassy slope towards the little fire the new men had burning, around which they had gathered to brew tea.

THE MORNING DAMP ON THE PADDOCKS was rising white in the sunshine when John Batman emerged from the treeline with his great-coat dragging over the growth, his arms full of bits of bark and grass. He passed the store shed and the shambles still rigged with two lonely hanging ewe's hocks and sat himself on the ground by the cook fire the men had burning. Black Bill was there, and Pigeon and John Crook of the Parramatta, all crouched at the coals drinking tea in tin mugs. Their dark faces studied Batman as he worked the bark hulls he'd been carrying out flat. They soon saw what he was about and John Crook reached into the fire's gut and sorted through the coals for something of use to Batman. He placed a few choice embers on the bark and on the moss spread there and Batman rolled the coals and the bark into one long cudgel which he bound up with twists of grass.

On the other side of the fire stationed away from the blacks the assignees studied the goings-on but it meant nothing to them. They picked at the boils infesting their necks and stared.

John Batman blew into the opening and called the coals into life. They'd taken no breakfast but the smokes above the hill put an urgency into Batman's planning.

On yer feet, he said.

The Dharug men led the party away from the farmhouse around the curves of the plains where the unburnt ground was dressed in saplings and the bracken grew as plush as grass. They made along the boundary of Kingston, tracking beside the wall of forest that rose sheer from the fields, until they reached the rim of Batman's holdings. Here the stands of gums in blossom, the fiddlebacked acacias and the gauntly made myrtles blanketed the hillside as far as they could see. It was a stretch of forest entirely hostile to folk of any nation, native or not. That beggarly clutch hung in rags and animal pelts and toting rusted firearms walked that ground as if pilgrims guided by the word of a demented god.

...

It was a hard slog that first morning. The terrain was overgrown and snow stood in the shadows lingering from winter. It was through old country they went, a thousand generations black. They walked hours up foothills and down gutters, passing through a draw of conifer stags burned out by wildfire where a raw wind stirred the branches. They wound through a gully strewn with charcoal that they crushed under their feet.

In the distance the southern approach of Ben Lomond rose out of the forest clefts, its bald peak noosed in clouds, and they followed the Parramatta men ever towards it. Around noon they stopped to eat. Tree ferns made a vault overhead and the men crouched at their bases scraping leeches from their feet and waiting for food. William Gould had a bag of smoked meat for their breakfast which he distributed to every man until he had one last strip remaining.

Give it to Black Bill over there, Batman said.

Horsehead pulled his lip back in disgust. Why dont he eat them boots instead, he said.

Bill worked the meat around as he leaned on his gun, the ligaments of his jaw flexing, his gaze on the old cur crouched across from him. He passed a water canteen back and forth with the Dharugs and spat mouthfuls, darkening the stones. They lingered a moment longer in the stand of tree ferns as the assigned men rebound their feet and once more lurched into the scrub.

. . .

Now they pushed through regions of landslip where fallen trees lay mouldering in their furrows and saplings sprouted along the very boughs of the fallen. The rovers mounted those logs one after another and felt the sun on their heads before crossing again into the cold forest cavity. They walked up a talus and over runs of cragged stone burst forth from the earth like filthy cuspids, stones that foreshadowed the dolerite stacks of the mountain looming in their vision. As they slogged up and down corrugations in the country Horsehead fell in alongside Jimmy Gumm and spoke into his ear.

Dont let that cat's turd get away with it, he said.

With what?

Givin you a beltin that's what.

Gumm looked around at him.

I mean a boy like that. It aint right.

Up ahead John Batman turned to take a summary of his party. Horsehead was quiet for a few yards. But when Batman continued on he spoke again. Us old hands ought to learn him some respect.

I dont need yer help, said Gumm.

No, I dont reckon you do.

I'll see it done meself.

There's bugger-all to him. Just careful you dont kill the wretch.

They filed on down a wooded swale where the groundcover dragged at their skins. Jimmy Gumm leaned in to speak in a whisper. When the moment presents I will have after him. You watch me back all right?

My oath I will.

But not until it presents, you hear.

. . .

37

They walked all day and deep into the afternoon. As the circular sun carved into the hills they came to a shallow rock face which Batman bade them scale, one pulling up another until all stood on top. They scanned the stretch of country rolling around the bend in the earth away below. It was a sheet of bluish green. The native hunting grounds made a patchwork of that textured expanse where the grasslands showed through and the herds of kangaroo could be seen, turning as one upon the pastures.

What had the men's attention though was not the country but a twist of smoke hung straight in the still air, a few miles distant to the east of the mountain. Those unquiet faces staring. A cloud shadow crossed the forest like the silhouette of a ship's hull moving over the seabed. They lowered each other down the rocks, making what they could of any handholds until their feet hit the hard ground once more. But Black Bill stayed on that lookout. Glaring at the crawl of white smoke etched large against the blue he was sucking a gum leaf between his lips until in time the men called him down, and he turned away to join them.

THEY MADE CAMP AS THE LIGHT drained from the sky and it was a miserable camp set beneath a mountain pine that had grown around a rock and split in half. A copse of candlebarks grew nearby, aged like rheumatic fingers and thickly boled. Moss crept up almost everything and the fust of dead wood and mould filled the nostrils; mushrooms as round and white as skulls glowed otherworldly in the shadows.

They piled up wood in the lee of that strange pine and Batman made a fire from his firestick and blew, banking wood on top. The assignees unwound the crusted bindings from their feet and placed the rags near the fire to dry, and in the throw of firelight the men hauled out their portions of flour and added a pound or so each to a communal damper that William Gould kneaded on a slab of bark. A wind picked up and no one spoke but each of them listened to the darkened forest beyond and clutched their loaded firearms across their laps. Soon Black Bill took himself from beside the fire and sat with Pigeon and

Crook where they shared a pipe at a small remove from the rest. Bill stretched his legs out before him and in turn hollowed his cheeks sucking on the stem.

How you come by them boots, friend? Horsehead was looking at him.

Through honest labour. Friend. He spoke around the pipe in his mouth and the words came as white balls that pilled and dissipated.

Huntin your own kind for bounty aint no sort of honest I know.

You ought to shut your mouth about honest I reckon, said John Batman. A crim like you.

Better born a crim than a bloody orang-outan.

Batman leaned forward. I aint above cutting yer tongue out. My word I aint.

Horsehead rolled back his shirt sleeves as if to demonstrate his credentials for just such a life and the firelight showed up the mare's head inked into his pale prison forearm, baring its teeth, its mane streaming in the wind. His hands were inked over in outlandish devices amassed from the netherparts of the globe, some faded and ill-defined and others freshly needled into his skin. A silence stole over the camp as the assignees chewed their tobacco and gazed at those tattoos.

The boy was first to speak. He looked at Batman. Have you bin this way before?

I have, said Batman.

The boy squinted through the faint rain that was now falling. Come after blacks was you?

Bushrangers. Batman was shining like some river creature hauled freshly ashore as the wet leather of his greatcoat gave back the flames and he looked around at Baxter. Welshman, he said. More wood.

There were a few moments of smoke and spark from the fire.

But there's more than bushrangers out here, continued Batman. There's the clans. A good many.

Can you find em?

Batman stared at the boy. Be sure of it.

And if we dont find no blacks, we'll just haul that one there in and be done with it, said Horsehead and he cocked his thumb in Bill's direction.

Black Bill was by the split pine, keeping out of the rain. In his hands was the longbladed dagger he wore behind his neck. It was inscribed over in spiral patterns by means of a steel burin and honed viciously keen on a width of east coast sandstone. He turned the dagger point on his palm and kept his hat brim low so that his face receded in the shadows. They all watched him.

What sort a damn ignorance makes you think we could haul him somewheres he hadnt a mind to go? said John Batman.

Horsehead spat on the fire. I seen him with Bickle. He aint much frolic.

What he is or what he aint aint for you to say.

41

I know what I see.

And that is all you know. I guarantee you. If you was to draw a bead on him, what do you think would happen? You think he'd stick up his hands?

Horsehead sat in silence. Glowered.

Pay attention to me now cause I'll tell you what. He'll run you from balls to breakfast with that there blade of his. Spill yer innermosts over the stones before you so much as draw down the cock.

The Vandemonian replaced the knife into the leather sheath strung between his shoulders and he tipped his hat on an angle to better meet the eyes of the assignees gazing at him across the wavering heat of the fire.

A black man raised white, said Batman. Think upon that fact. Not a day passing where some slander aint spoken in his presence. How many times you suppose he has defended hisself? I tell you somethin else. He keeps account. I seen him break a man's arm twelve months after the fact. This fellow had once drawn a blade against Bill, but he wont draw nothin again God help him.

Horsehead spat a string of tobacco liquor onto the fire where it hissed and raised a stink like charring hair.

I reckon even halfwits like you gang of dirts know of the Man Eater, said Batman.

The men nodded at mention of Jeffries.

You'll likely have heard tell it was John Darke what finally caught him, said Batman.

They nodded once more.

John Darke I was told by some, said Gumm. But Jeffries give himself up. Boneless coward that he was.

That aint the strict truth of the matter, said Batman. He was pursued by several parties but it was him, Black Bill there, caught the monster.

Him?

The selfsame.

The Vandemonian leaned forward and flung the dregs from his mug over the fire. His wet clothes clung to him. I was a party to the taking of Jeffries, he said. But merely a party.

The Man Eater told me it was you took him, said Batman. I was there too dont forget.

Under the gaze of the eight men Bill filled his mug from the billycan. Rain fell from the limbs above, fell and vanished in the fire's gut. They watched him crush a gum leaf into his tea and then stir it with a long black finger. A good many things come out of his mouth, he said. But for the most part they were lies or worse. I will tell you this much though. Then Bill began upon a history he'd recounted a thousand times in grog shops and stock huts and walking the trails of the back country.

I saw her with my own honest eyes, he said above the popping of the fire. A woman hardly older than you, boy. Blackened about her eyes, missing her front teeth, bleeding and staggering and near enough to naked she was. Crying as if she never meant to stop. Something truly awful had visited her for which

she had no words to tell. I never saw its like. I was raised in the house of James Cox, Esquire, raised as good as blood, raised alongside his own children. I saw a good many things in my life there but now I was seeing something wholly new. When this woman arrived at the house she was tended by Mr. Cox's maid and given rum and water for the pain and put to bed. Come the following day she'd regained herself somewhat but more was the pity for her.

I believed her deranged and I dont doubt even now that she was. I told Mr. Cox and he was inclined to agree but nonetheless we went to her room and tried to get some sense from her. In the darkened room where she tolerated no light and where she was hidden among the bedclothes with her face covered over she commenced to tell us her story. And Mr. Cox and I, we listened and scarcely believed what we heard.

Bill paused in his storytelling and drank from his mug of tea. The rain was easing and the thudding on his hat had slowed. He raked his eyes across them.

Two men—Jeffries and a companion—had fallen upon this woman's hut and upon her family, he said, but to hear her describe them we thought they were devils set forth from the core of the earth all ablaze and bent on blood spill. Most of what come out was barely more than nonsense but what I heard, what I understood at least, stopped the marrow in my bones.

Seems these men entered her hut in the evening. They had

hold of a servant belonged of her neighbour and held a pistol to his head. They entered the hut where were sitting the woman and her husband and her infant and they screamed like animals and bade the householders to stay down. They knelt that old servant man among the child's toys and proceeded to release the hammer. I saw his body when it was buried. The whole front of his head shot clean away. The woman's clothes were rank with gore even a week later. Then a second pistol was produced and the husband was shot.

The lags were unmoved by the tale. They pulled their blankets around and wiped their faces as the rain ran off their hair.

Bill nodded, continued. Aye. If that was the worst, surely you'd sleep the night and wake come sunrise and never think again upon the Man Eater. But I have not finished. Not yet at least. So he marched that woman from her hut at pistolpoint while his partner sacked the place for food. The infant wailing in her arms. And he snatched the child's leg and tore the child away and to hear this woman tell it he tore the very blood from her beating heart. He tore that child away and set to dashing it against a gum tree and all that sad scrub was filled with the sound.

The company was silent as the Vandemonian swirled his tea and stared into the dark fluid as if he might there find an answer or at least find a question worth his breath. He swirled the tea and swallowed and went on.

Having been marched a dozen miles by Jeffries and his partner and having suffered their depraved attentions over some
days, the woman made her escape by chewing through her
bindings in the black of night. Her husband had survived his
wounds but even the living sight of him seemed no great comfort to her and it was some time before Mr. Cox's maid was able
to move her from that bed. I sat with her a good long while and
listened to her ramblings and I came to know the Man Eater
by his deeds and to see him outlined in my mind. So when Mr.
Cox put together a party intended to track the pair, I was the
very first to put myself forward. Our own Mr. Batman organ-
ised a party too, after hearing my account of the matter.

John Batman nodded. It was meself, William Gould there
and another fellow, Smith.

What did they have on his head? said Howell Baxter.

Ten pound and yer ticket.

Ten pound?

Ten. And I tell you, wasnt a scoundrel in the district thinkin
of nothin else.

Black Bill observed this exchange with dark and unblinking eyes. When a fresh silence descended upon the campsite he
spoke again.

It was Mr. Darke found the Man Eater when perchance he
saw him skitter in the trees around the flanks of his farmhouse.
Jeffries put into the scrub and lost Darke along the gullied
banks of the Nile where no sort of bushman could lose his

quarry. Tracks stay a week in the soft earth there and will even confide the frame and height of the mark for those adept at the reading of it. But Darke is no sort of bushman. No sort at all. I was in Mr. Cox's party who set out with Darke that evening.

Jeffries wasted no effort hiding his trace and it ran so plainly we went at a trot and followed the tracks without danger of losing them. All night we followed and we arrived at a lonely stock hut as the sun was staining the sky and we found inside some of Mr. Darke's men sleeping off a skinful of rum. You could smell the reeking even outside the hut. Mr. Darke called them out as drunkards and promised floggings for all and raged until a bottle was handed his way. He partook of a dram and then it was himself splayed out between them, necking from the bottle and sleeping through the freezing dawn.

The men had their ears bent listening to Bill's tale and when he paused to take a sip of his tea they also raised their mugs and drank. The Vandemonian flicked a finger at the billycan in the fire for another serving and the boy obliged by lifting it away with a stick and pouring using his sleeve tugged over his fingers against the burning handle. With a fresh steaming mug in his hands Bill went on and the men listened now like he was giving scripture.

Jeffries was nearby for sure. I read his trace past the hut and off aways. I surveyed the shifting weather and scouted Jeffries' trace some hundred yards onto Mill's Plain. As I was running my eye across the line of trees I saw him, dressed in a long dark coat of leather and wending through the gaunt scrub. To my eyes he was wholly unnatural in that landscape. So I shouldered my weapon and drew a sight on him.

Bill pulled on his tea. I could have struck him, he said. No doubt in my mind. But if I missed he was off once more into the wilds and gone. I had to be sure, you see. For that reason I returned to the hut and woke Mr. Darke and the others and they come half dressed and stinking drunk and we surrounded the Man Eater before he knew it. One of Darke's men was up to him first and presented his gun to Jeffries, which reduced him to grovelling of the most pitiful sort. They beat him and kicked him and stomped him. Even Mr. Darke, even Mr. Cottrell the constable. I stopped them; if I hadnt surely one more murder would have been committed.

That Man Eater, he was a sorry wretch. Sorry of sight and sorry of deed. They turned out his pockets and what do you suppose they found? You know well and good what they found. An arm severed at the elbow. Rancid and chewed up. It was belonged of his partner murdered cruelly in his sleep. That was a revelation to harden the most amiable among the hunting party. One of Darke's men urinated on the Man Eater's bare skin and a knife was pressed to his shoulder and someone screamed that he would be served his own fried arm for breakfast. The Man Eater was hysterical. They beat him out cold. Then he was roped and dragged naked to Mr. Cox's residence and that's how it was done. How he was caught.

The boy spoke up. You oughta of killed him.

Would you have?

My bloody oath, said the boy.

Then you would have hanged alongside him. Bill turned and looked across the selection of gaunt faces. I took my leave from Darke for fear of being a party to murder and I fell in the following day with the Leetermairremener, who are a kind people. Around their hearth fire we gathered and I ate their possum and offered my tobacco and I told the story of the Man Eater and the slaughter he so freely countenanced. The old men of the tribe allowed me measure to speak and called me son and smoked my tobacco but I was clothed as a white man and they understood me as white. They listened and nodded as I spoke and the children hid from me behind their mothers. Some of their retinue wore shirts or trousers looted from stock huts and they had a single flintlock which was rusted all but useless and I believe they thought themselves versed in the comings and goings of whitefolk, but as they listened to the awful tale I told, the old men of the tribe grew into the knowledge that their solitary ways were ever closer to being undone.

They waited for Bill to go on but he drew on his tea and listened to the trees groan like the damned and presently they understood that his tale had finished.

No more was said. The wind shearing through the campsite drove the company men deeper into their blankets for refuge. By now the rain had ceased but the ground was sodden, except at the base of the thickest trees, and they contorted themselves between these roots for shelter. Darkness lay beyond the firelight and their eyes burned as they scrutinised that formless sweep of black. Nine men cloistered among the recesses, as cold and dulled as stones. What might be conceived of as a measure of men was for them a simple paucity. For that which moaned inside them was given no idiom to show itself.

. . .

Black Bill awoke to the prodding of a bare foot, cold and split-nailed in the fireless dark. He pushed his hat from his eyes. A figure stood over him training a weapon upon the square of his chest. The other men slept a dead sleep and stirred not a wink when Horsehead, with his consumptive's wheeze, drew down the hammer on his piece, the unoiled creak of it like floorboards giving.

Hand us them boots, darkie, he growled.

The Vandemonian pushed back his blankets and tenderly raised himself up.

Horsehead was shrouded in his own blankets and his breath showed in the void between the two men as he spoke. You got no need of em.

Black Bill slid against the tree he'd been sleeping under and rose to his full height. From behind his neck he drew his dagger, the blade held downwards. He waited and stared. In the silence Horsehead made no move nor did he release the hammer. He was in a bind: firing would wake Batman and Batman was likely to respond in kind. Bill raised the blade alongside his cheek from where he might better strike a blow.

It was a long instant as the pair stood off like dogs and the ragged snores of the company men came from the darkness. Bill clenched his fist upon the bone handle.

Horsehead went backwards a pace and wheezed at the Vandemonian, I'm takin to the bush. I dont want no part of this madness. Now givem here. Elsewise I'll finish you with ball. He watched the Vandemonian's blade wink and he studied that hardened face for evidence of fear or doubt but all he beheld was clear intent.

He moved back another pace, then another. At length Horsehead lowered the mouth of his gun, but even as he rested the weapon upon a tree root and raised his hand to signal for calm the Vandemonian kept his knife bared. Eventually the assigned man sat himself beside his gun and tugged his damp blankets across his legs like some shabby squatter taking his ease.

Keep the bloody things then, he said.

Black Bill pulled his hat brim low and stared at the creature hunched down beside the fire, shivering beneath his bedding. And he watched that figure until the sun flowered behind the horizon.

ALL THAT NEXT MORNING THEY FOLLOWED where the Parramatta men led, going over the rough underscrub sorely and without enthusiasm. To the rear John Batman followed with his gun crooked over one arm, watching every movement of the scrub as if it meant him ill. The shoeless men slipped down the banks and mossed chines, struggling through their long task without a break. Their empty guts cramped up and they hounded Batman for food but he would not be swayed. In the hour before noon they cut across a markener snaking through the bush that had been hacked by clans passing around the mountain. It was a fine track that followed the mountain's swells and hollows and Pigeon considered both courses a moment, the other men watching him at his deliberations. He waved the mosquitoes from his neck, folded his arms across his chest. Then he led the party off along the markener's northern route. The markener had not seen fire in many a year; at one time it had been wide enough for two men abreast but now it was narrowed into archways of sinewed leatherwoods and in the light wells young shrubs of every sort swallowed up the path and clawed at their clothes. The bush was festooned with leeches like gaping black worms reaching from the branches and as the men walked they plucked them from their skin and burst them between their fingers.

In the afternoon they moved up through thinner groves of rainforest and through squatly grown tree ferns and their pace picked up. John Batman took up whistling a broken tune which dipped and rose across the same few bars over and over as they strode along; the emus he raised with that sound crashed off among the trees in threes and fours, booming deep down their throats in alarm. Somewhere a lone crow called. A few more miles around the swollen base of Ben Lomond they crossed a stand of black gum, towering like immense stone pillars. The company men climbed over the roots and tipped their heads back to study the ironcoloured sky labouring past the crests of those trees. The uppermost branches stirred as long gusts full of the cold of the southern ice lands flowed through. The men moved around those colossal gums, watching the rotting turf that shifted with the little scurrying life, but they had not got far before Black Bill held aloft his hat and brought the party to a halt. He was stood with his six-foot fowler trained on the trees and he raised a finger for silence. The company men waited.

tawattya, Bill called but it soaked into the forest, lost amid the bird cry.

In the near distance was a ring of temma. They were built on loose uneven soil but the clans had little ground now to choose from, as Batman had the best of it for his sheep. Bill approached each of the temma in turn, calling, and peering inside. He stepped over a dead hearth fire strewn about with the shattered bones of wallabies, their fur and dark signs of blood and he held his hand above the coals a moment then tipped back his hat at an angle. The party men emerged and moved guardedly into the village with their weapons to their shoulders, studying the stretchings of bush that led off away eastwards around Ben Lomond. Away from the temma, piles of scat lay cast over with handfuls of grass caked in wipings and the Dharugs nudged at the turds with the points of their toes. Blackening, hard, juiceless. Crook pinched a clod in his fingers and it split open. Wet inside still. They were not long departed. He showed Bill.

Two days gone, said Bill. Not more.

Batman gazed up at the mountain. Two?

Not more.

Aye. Well then.

...

They took a spell there, kneeling among the native huts. Out of his drum Batman produced an apple, a perfect red apple, and quartered it with his skinning knife. Liquid ran clear over

54

his knuckles and he sucked them clean and then laid the segments neat before him where they glistened under the gaze of eight men.

I never had apple before, the boy said.

Batman gave a quarter to every man and the fellow beside him to divide how they saw. Howell Baxter and Jimmy Gumm halved a quarter widthways and ate it. Black Bill placed his segment in his creamy palm and looked at the boy.

Have it, he said.

Without a word the boy snatched the apple and stuffed the lump sideways in his mouth. He resembled the beggar children in the back alleys of Launceston, those tiny souls stealing food from households and pleading coins from passers-by. Bill had given them his pennies and his last wedge of bread and then his blanket. They'd thanked him and asked if he was a nigger and he'd replied that he was a Vandemonian born and grown; they'd nodded like old weathered sages and shaken his hand. They stank of the muck of the towns and their eyes loomed too large in their skulls.

What's he done? said the boy.

He? said Bill.

This witch.

Boy, what is your name?

Thomas Toosey.

You shouldnt be here, Thomas.

Well I know he done somethin.

Dont concern yourself with it.

The boy jutted his head at the armed men settled there-abouts. It is my concern though, aint it.

Bill allowed that point. He did as we all do, he said.

Did what?

No more questions. You are a boy.

I'm fifteen.

The boy licked apple juice off his fingers. Black Bill took up a handful of leaves and let them fall. The leaves turned wounded spirals.

He's just a man is all.

There was more the boy wanted to ask and he showed it by shifting his weight to get a better view of Bill's face. The shred-ded sunlight through the trees cast them over in speckling, as if they were fish lying idle in shallows. But Black Bill stood up and walked off, leaving the boy alone with his questions.

. . .

The temma were woven from slabs of bark laid over a frame of curved branches that had been jammed into the earth. Skins covered the earthen floors inside, the whole teeming with fleas. As he tossed through each hut for things of worth Black Bill upended a hessian sack. A hand mirror, half a bro-ken teacup patterned with prancing horses, an empty jam tin, a broad red book. Nothing of any value or use to a mob

of wandering clansfolk. He reached down for the book where it lay.

A Bible. As sturdy as firewood in his hand. He turned the damp pages one by one and every page, every column of text, every inch of every surface was inked with arcane circles, spirals, in bloodred ochre. The broken halves of the words hanging between those scrawls were rendered useless. Whatever authority the volume had held was muted by those fierce curls and angles, shapes echoed in the very build of the world. He closed the book and tossed it on the dead fire.

Jimmy Gumm was likewise engaged in plundering and he watched Bill throw that blemished Bible aside. He snatched the book from the ashes and tucked it inside his drum where he'd also stashed a native shell necklace, a sarcenet ribbon and a hairbrush of turned whalebone and boar bristles. He resettled the weight of the bag across his shoulder and nodded at the Vandemonian who was stood at rest in a warm sun streak.

It'll do for wipin me fundament, he said.

In the forest shadows Horsehead drew up beside Jimmy Gumm and leaned slightly into him. His vagrant's face was gathered in a scowl. He spoke hotly on Gumm's neck. He's by hisself.

Gumm nodded. He smoothed down his beard, unlooped the drum from over his head and set it down. His hands clenched in two broad fists as he spoke to Horsehead.

Watch them others dont get wind of this. Till I'm done at least.

. . .

The boy was squatting in the ferns near the outermost of the native shanties with his trousers bunched about his knees. Flies crawled along his legs and he brushed them away but they rose and returned as before. He shat quietly on the ground then plucked coarse bracken fronds, crushed them into a ball and dabbed at his hole. He was reaching for a second handful when Jimmy Gumm emerged from behind a silver wattle, glancing

58

over his shoulder before coming forward. He gestured at the boy and looked away.

Stand up now. Take the hidin that's comin to ye.

The boy hiked up his trousers and moved back. His leavings steamed in the ferns between them. He retied the cord of his pants. What hidin?

The one I owe.

The boy looked around but there were none present save the wattles. He drew himself up and pushed out his jaw.

It's a matter of my dignity and what you done to it, said Gumm.

You brokeheaded old fumbler. How's a lag like you got any dignity?

That's enough out ayou.

Gumm lumbered forward and grabbed him. For an instant he had the boy by the sleeve and was bringing his fist about to crack him in the teeth but the boy was too sly. He snatched his arm away and jumped outside the line of the punch, countering with his own. It struck Gumm square in the throat. He gagged, closed his eyes and stumbled but the boy was on him now, kicking at his groin and driving his awkward fists into the side of his head. The bigger man dropped onto his rear and the boy stood back with his fists raised as Gumm grasped his throat, coughing. Gumm rolled over in the bracken and bits of bark and muck clung to his clothes. On all fours he looked up at the boy and winced. He tried to speak but could not.

From behind the great flutes of a blue gum two men slumped, holding each other, their faces squeezed up as they cackled like beaten cats. Tears leaked down the slates of their cheeks. Gumm lowered his head.

Oh, said Horsehead. Oh he's done it to you again. Oh dear oh dear oh deary me.

Baxter threw back his head and howled from deep down inside his long frame. A madman's guffaw.

You miserable bastards, said Gumm through his hoarse throat.

But it only had them laughing the harder.

THE EARTH WAS A MESS OF tracks where natives had come and gone for days but Pigeon and Crook went about bent over in diagnosis until they agreed that the natives had decamped eastwards in number. Black Bill considered the trail, running his hat brim through his fingers. The Parramatta men were gone off into the scrub and Bill fell in behind them as they picked out the way and led the company onwards after whatever faint trace they saw there. The air was full of the sound of their passing: the creak of boots, the sweeping of branch against thigh. They curved over a rise and down a slight shaded gully where it banked and the damp earth turned under their bare or booted or bandaged feet. Here the men drank from a creek that sputtered along the gully floor and they filled their canteens from a rockpool set about with tree ferns. The sun above was dimmed by the canopy and in the halflight the mosquitoes swarmed upon their naked parts so that every hand they raised sent up a flotilla, mindless, maddening, until it forced them to move on once more.

Mid-afternoon Crook started singing. He chanted as he walked, an unelaborate tune rising and falling upon a rhythm only the whitebanded and ochred men of the Dharug understood. Black Bill heard in it the echo of the crow shrike and the chiming of the quail-thrush, the age-old song of an arid land. Pigeon joined his voice to it and those two sounded out their chorus upon the landscape as the party men looked about in cold disdain or shook their heads.

Then Jimmy Gumm found voice too. Flecks of spit caught in his beard as he sang. Good people what will you of all be bereft? Will you never learn wit whilst a penny is left?

All the colonials knew that tune. Even Batman, who had never placed a foot upon English soil in his life. They sang together. We're all like the dog in the fable betrayed, to let go our substance and snap at the shade!

And so Crook's song coalesced into one discordant wail with the ballad, the amalgamation ringing around the mountainside like the death cry of some misbegotten beast, while Black Bill quietly studied the sheer gorge they walked through.

. . .

Late in the afternoon as the sun burst on the horizon in an outward copper spread Pigeon crouched at a grass embankment, his fingertips caressing the face of the earth in that long light.

First mob come up ere, said Pigeon. He pointed out the marks.

A few yards away the grass rose upwards into scrub again and Pigeon walked nearer, watching the ground as he went, his forehead creasing. He paused at the grass edge and pinched the flattened stalks to reckon the passing of time. Charcoaled tree husks intermingled with the living where a fire had burnt through some years back. The squeeze of black gum and pine was looser here and the scrub was easily covered on foot, save for the many saplings germinated in the blaze; these whipped their legs and caught them up.

Second mob come that way, he said and gestured down the mountainside. All go together. One big bloody mob now them buggers.

Batman eased the cork from his quart flask and poured a measure into his open mouth. They watched him survey that country where it rolled away down the slope towards the blue-hued mountains in the south masked by a haze. The dark shapes of hawks crawled across the clouds. He removed his hat, his hair crowned in where the hoop had sat.

Seems we'll be made to earn our payment, he said.

Plenty dogs. Plenty kids too, said Pigeon.

Horsehead raised his eyes at this, his pale features a mess of wrinkling and his mouth hard set. Kids? he said.

Batman drew another mouthful.

The light was thinning. Pigeon strode into the scrub where he was followed by the roving party coming ever slower for want of rest and food. The wide trodden trail led them past swamp gums hung with long bark spools that turned in the breeze. All of them walking with heads down as the sun withdrew behind the mountain's dripping wax crags, wheeling along its ancient gutter downwards into the underworld.

...

An hour along the trail they tasted wood smoke upon the wind. The bush was a grim assemblage of shadows by now and the chirruping and howling of night creatures grew bolder as the light evaporated. The Parramatta men picked out a path among the trees where the party would not be seen. Batman allowed no speaking nor spitting and Pigeon and Crook mutely gestured to guide the men on. To still the rattling locks of their weapons the assignees stuffed gum leaves under the mechanisms. Batman and Bill quieted their boot soles with kangaroo hide. Where the path narrowed the men drew into single file and their passing was evidenced by little more than the whisper of the understorey as it closed behind them.

Before that hour had ended all of the company could see the blinking fires in the scrub away down the slope. It was a sight that tested their resolve. From the banks of a fold they surveyed the land south. The stubs of firelight glistened in the dark of the forest. As the men of the roving party stared across the moon-silvered bushscape, John Batman ordered them down. They crouched behind the trees and unslung their weapons. Among that company only Batman and Black Bill continued to watch the fires burning in the distance. Bill on his knees pulled off his hat as he tallied first the fires then the clansfolk around them. I make it ten fires, Bill whispered.

I see dog tracks by the fives of thousands, said Batman. They are some big lot.

Aye.

How many men you see? said Batman.

A good few.

Hazard a guess.

He was quiet a moment. Eighty, he said. A hundred.

Jimmy Gumm shook his head. And here's us nine.

The boy was squatting like a river toad in the weeds. Glad you give me a gun now, arent you? he said.

Nine will do, said John Batman. It will do superbly.

There drifted in the night air the sound of a story being danced around the bonfires, the sound of one voice performing for a hundred souls. A single clansman passed before the flames and that warrior with his coiled ropes of hair was distinguished in silhouette, treading out the shapes of his narrative. His song rising and mingling with the drifts of smoke. In the late darkness a cold descended and even wrapped in blankets the party men could not escape the bitterness. The Parramatta men so recently come from their dustlands seemed crippled with it and sat huddled together, silent and rigid. Only Bill forwent his blanket. The jacket he wore was

thin but if he was cold he made no show of it. He was cleaning the gunblack from the pan of his oversized fowler. It was a
venerable old piece hooded with possum hide to keep the lock
dry. He wiped out the pan with the edge of his shirt, primed it
for firing and replaced the hood.

What's he singin about down there? the boy said to him.

Keep yer voice down, said Batman.

We ought to just get down there, the boy said. Surprisem in
the dark.

Lad, if you had any sense of what's comin you wouldnt be in
no hurry for it. Batman was stretched out at rest beneath his
hat and his eyes remained closed as he spoke.

The boy watched him. He hugged his knees up and looked
away.

...

At midnight Batman dug an oilcloth from his drum and set
the boy to polishing the pans and the boy bowed his head
over each mechanism as if he was whispering something
inside, fingering the cloth into the workings and drying the
parts. Batman took the cleaned pieces across his knee where
he tested the mating of lock and frizzen and when satisfied he
passed them off one by one to the assigned men. They readied
the weapons sorely slowly in the cold. John Batman, with his
doublebarrel gun on his shoulder and his two fists clenched

inside his greatcoat, stepped before the rovers and offered them what small words he had.

If you want them tickets of leave from the Governor, you'd best save some live head. Makes for good show bringin em in.

They saw the sense in it and said so.

On the approach they wove a path down the slope and Howell Baxter in his odd gait tumbled and muddied his clothes. They waited while Baxter found his feet and then Pigeon, Crook and Black Bill carried on towards the towering light of the native fires, forcing the rest to jog a few paces along the track cut by the passing of the clanspeople. Pigeon drew long lungfuls of air through his nose. Then he followed the westerly into the scrub downwind of the campsite and the rovers followed.

What Black Bill witnessed from that cover stayed with him all his days. A crowd of shining damp faces were gathered in the firelight and its shimmer picked out incisions raised on their chests and streaks of ochre they wore like costuming. Manalargena strode among the revellers and bellowed out his epic: a tale of animosity among clans and the requital he'd delivered for his people when his cousin's wife was carried off and he'd led men against the trespassers. He was naked, his greased skin aflame. He walked and he clapped and the singing rose around him into the sky as the voices praised their ancient dead. Above it all the full moon rolled like a blinded eye as Black Bill gripped the loaded fowling piece tighter.

They formed a line eight abreast. John Batman bade them to put the hammers on the cock and on that signal the strike of settling mechanisms sounded along their line. In formation they moved upon the two conferencing clans, wading through the loose packing of brush, their weapons at their shoulders. It was dogs scavenging at the edge of the campsite that started barking first, lean and boney mongrels working through the refuse where wallabies had been gutted. They bayed at the interlopers and the noise broke the headman from his narrative. As his singing waned into quiet talk the clansmen took up waddies and spears, peering into the scrub from where the roving party came on them like ascended deadmen, eerily pale, gaunt, ungraceful.

Tails of flame shaped the clansmen from the dark in a volley of shots and the bright gouts of their blood erupted. Two were felled, the others fled, the common squall of their cries sounding while the rovers repacked their weapons. Black Bill was first reloaded and first into the campsite, his eyes cutting every way. He shouldered past a stumbling woman, stalked deeper into the camp with his weapon trained on the ragged torn shadows cast by the fires. A great knot of people broke off before the party, naked women hauling naked children, young men as thinly boned as the spears they threw, the whole howling in one voice of consummate horror. Without thought the ruiners lay about themselves with the butts of their weapons, knocking down whoever strayed too near or firing into that mass unhindered.

Some of the clan ran through the fires to escape and some trampled the fallen where they screamed. An old man tottered as he held a wound in his ribs. Black Bill drew his knife but the fellow was lost and gone in the blind dark scrub and Bill moved off through the pall of sulfur after the headman.

It had become by now a scene of great misery. Wailing sounded in the bush beyond the firelight as the clansfolk decamped for the fastness of the mountain forest. The assignees followed the cries of which they had no understanding but Black Bill did and he knew parents called for children and wives for husbands and above it all was the war cry of men steeling to fight. They gave fire without discrimination into the body of stampeding people who fell all alike. The assignees stopped to reprime their weapons and fired on one knee or at a run and soon the drifts of gunsmoke choked the air and the blood trails tracked across the campsite shone in the light of the bonfires.

Black Bill stared along the barrel of his piece as he moved among the bark huts. Around the darkened edges of the village Pigeon and Crook skulked in a strange parody of the vanished clanspeople they hunted, grim and watchful. Bill went low past the rough dwellings and into the trees edging the village and here the screaming wounded could be heard between all the weapon fire. By the smokeblue moonlight Bill made out the headman carrying a child under each arm, bursting up the wooded slope in great strides. His greased skin showed in silver flashes between the trees as he ran and the children's legs bounced. The Vandemonian called him out with a hoarse roar. Manalargena stopped and turned and his white eyes loomed stark in his face as he called down to the Vandemonian, Tummer-ti makara!

Give yerself up.

milaythina nika.

Black Bill felt the belled muzzle buck as he fired. The report played out in the hills. Through the haze he saw the headman buckle but then right himself and the children screamed as he broke away for the mountain folds to the north, bearing them with him. Bill followed, pulling himself up the steep slope by handfuls of bracken and entering the gums after the headman. If there was blood it was lost in the dark. While the roar of firearms flattened behind him in the cold the Vandemonian studied the dogwood but he saw no trace of the headman. Bill came to a fallen tree in the scrub where a plush moss grew and covered the trunk entire. He felt along its surface for signs of disturbance but in that abysmal dark he saw barely where to place his hand. He stood and turned, listening over the beating of his heart. He heard nothing. All was still. He moved on another few hundred feet and crouched in the bushes and here he reprimed his weapon and dosed the pan from the powder bag. As he moved off there came a snivelling from further up the rise, then the clatter of underbrush. The children were clinging together among some burly knotted blue gum roots when he saw them. He came through the brush angling his body that he might approach unheard but when the children looked past him he knew himself outplayed. He aimed his fowling piece upon that clearing where long fissures of moonlight issued through the woven canopy but Manalargena fell on him from behind, assailing him across the neck with his great blackwood waddy. It pitched him forward, the gun knocked out of his reach, and Bill rolled up to face the headman where he stood holding the club above himself. He beat the waddy down upon Bill's upraised arms and hammered at him until the Vandemonian no longer fought but merely took the blows. Only then did he cease. Manalargena called the children to him and once more they made forth into the heavy bushlands around the mountain, joining a retinue of the desolate borne along in fear of the gunfire they heard coming back off the mountain.

In the night Bill's unborn son found him and ran a hand across his stubbled brown cheek. It woke Bill and he looked long into his son's face before he recognised it. At once he felt the ache in his bones and the misery of being lifted from his frame. It was overwhelming and his throat thickened as he asked his son how he'd found him here in foreign country.

I followed you, he said.

Bill was weeping. He held his son's shoulders close and in that grip he knew this was the right and true of the world, this warmth of bodies, this tightness of throat. Bill held his son and sobbed with sweet relief. It was over. He was freed. He raised the boy high to his shoulders where he gripped the ochred ropes of hair on his father's head like the reins of a carthorse. Together they walked.

. . .

The birdlife that rose with the sun chattered and stirred Black Bill awake. He was stretched out on the rot of the forest floor in the long shadows of dawn. He felt his misshapen jaw and the blood caked on his face and for a moment he lay back and emptied his gaze as if he was the last man on God's dying earth.

One of his teeth was loose. The first fingers of his left hand were plainly broken, hooked where they had been straight. He felt himself over and found the side of his head clagged with blood, his ears swollen badly and a gouge full of muck above his eye. He pushed himself upright. A few feet away his piece lay where it had fallen, dusted in dirt, and he used it to stand.

The bonfires were burning yet and the glow led him into the campgrounds once more. Dogs paced before the fires, masterless, turning in chaotic gangs that neither began nor ended but ran always together. Bill leaned on his gun and surveyed the scene from some cover at the edge of the clearing. So many dogs that the shadows seethed with them. Nothing else moved in that devastation save the steady whipping of flames, so he moved forward into the rising sunlight, and sat himself down to wait for John Batman.

. . .

Soon one person and another and another emerged from the bush. Ominous figures, rifles borne in their arms. They did not cooee but came cautiously into the clearing through the smoke billows. The dog packs parted and closed behind them. Some growled but this the men disregarded and kept on towards the few scattered temma where Black Bill was crouched observing their progress. He rose from his position and walked the length of the camp to meet them.

In his hands Batman held a length of rope and at the end of it was a young girl. The rope was tied around her neck and she did not resist but followed where he hauled her. The child she carried in her arms was equally meek and she clutched it to her chest as she stumbled along behind Batman. They were three where eight had gone. Batman and Jimmy Gumm and the boy. All moving at pace and glancing frequently to the rear, they approached the fires, dropped their knapsacks and knelt to repack the barrels of their weapons.

Some bastard's followin, said Batman. Watch them trees there.

The two assignees glanced around at the scrub and at Bill where he stood armed and damaged and they drew their weapons tightly to their shoulders.

What's happened to you then? said Gumm as he studied the Vandemonian.

But Bill only spat blood on the ashes.

Hold her, said Batman.

He passed over the lead rope and took hold of the girl as if she were a cull ewe. He forced her head to the ground and Bill looped a hitch around her feet so that she was barely given slack to breathe. Her dark eyes widened as the rope drew taut. Batman made to pry the child from her arms but the girl held on with a fierceness that had the child near to ripping apart and he wailed all the more loudly for it. The awful sound had Batman soon relenting and the child was left howling and holding his mother. Batman reached for his fowling piece, eased his knee from the girl's back.

Dont know no modesty does she, said the boy. He gazed at the half apples of her breasts.

Are you hearin me? Watch them trees.

I'm doin that.

The Plindermairhemener girl was tall and thin and her child was much of a kind with her. Her patterned scars were dabbed over with ochre and she was otherwise painted up for a ceremony she would never undergo. Her scalp was freshly shaved and bloody scabs showed where the scallop shell had dug too deep. Bill crouched beside her and put out his hand to the crying child. The girl called out.

What's she sayin? said Gumm.

Bill looked up at him. Help me.

Christ, he said, you'd swear she was bein skinned. He rubbed his eyes with thumb and forefinger. Then he brought his gun up. I seen somefink, he said.

He pointed to the smoke drift and the ghostly line of swamp gums behind it. John Batman scanned those trees and he also perhaps saw some form of what Gumm had seen because he signalled to take cover behind a fallen tree, a massive thing of two hundred feet or more. The men found cover behind its mossy bulk and propped their pieces upon it, watching the trees around the clearing. On the open ground the girl lay struggling at her bindings. She raised her voice once more in a plaintive cry to her clansfolk.

Take care and dont shoot Pigeon or Crook neither, said Batman.

Bill cupped his shattered fingers as he watched the treeline. I've no ball left, he said to Batman.

Just keep yer head down then.

I see one.

Where?

Over there, said Bill. You see it?

I dont see nothin.

There.

Batman narrowed his eyes. By that rock you mean?

Aye, that's it.

Bugger me, you've the eyes of a needlemaker.

Batman pressed his cheek to the small of the stock, took sight of the underscrub and released the cock. The thunderclap caused the girl to cease her mournful calling and there came from the bush opposite the sounds of men.

Dont shoot you bastards, we're white.

They lowered their weapons as the remnants of the roving party appeared in the campsite. They stumbled past the bald, rounded temma and vaulted the fallen tree to join the company men in the cover it afforded. John Batman offered a flask of water and the newcomers drank and wiped their whiskers backhanded. Pigeon and Crook were the last into camp, the last into cover. They refused the water flask and remained standing and watchful where the others seemed content to rest. John Batman put questions to his servant Gould as the assignees checked the wrappings on their feet.

See any?

A good few.

Put them down, did you?

I shot up near on a pound of powder. I saw a deal of blood. More than that I cant say.

Howell Baxter shook the mud from his bindings and rewrapped his feet. When he spoke his fathomless voice was full of the same weary ache they all felt. But that mongrel Horsehead, he said. He's gone and disa-bloody-peared somewheres.

...

It was the Vandemonian who finally went to see about the girl and her child. He poured a measure of water down her throat and wrapped the child in a possum skin. She had no broil left and sipped the water he offered. Her damp eyes closed. Black Bill corked the canteen, stood and returned to the company. The Dharugs were sharing a pipe and they offered the stem to Black Bill. The smoke rose and filtered through the feathered fronds of the wattles parasoled above them. Bill pulled a turn on the pipe before Pigeon slipped the pipe back into his own mouth, clattering it along his teeth to and fro.

I dont see no dead ones nowheres, said the boy. He was looking across the barren campfield. Where you spose they went?

We didnt kill none, said Jimmy Gumm.

But I saw em fall.

Gumm held up a pouch of shot. This weight wouldnt knock the grin off a halfwit. Wastin our powder, we are.

That weight'll do what we need, said Batman, and he tipped back his hat and stared.

If you need them blacks mighty startled it will. If you need em killed use decent ball I say.

Batman raised his doublebarrel gun and the wide-bored holes were two sightless eyes which he brought to bear on Gumm. Well hows abouts you stand up and tell me how startled you get, he said.

Jimmy Gumm ground his jaw, his loose eye gazing offwards. I was just sharin me opinion.

An opinion worth less than the spit you made it with. Now I'll shoot every last black hide on this mountain and be glad for it but if you want yer ticket you'll take in some live head with me. Batman lowered his weapon.

They had a meagre breakfast squatting there at the fires, gathered where the sun had chased away the shadows and the frost. William Gould passed around a damper nub which they broke into and shared. Every man of that company watched the scrub flanks and the stands of man ferns for the clansfolk that they supposed at any moment would fall upon them, yabbering in tongues and waving their spears, but no such events occurred. Instead, the sky held firmly blue and the sun beamed warm on them as they slurped their tea. The girl was roped up spitting distance from the fire where they were cooking, her animal skins askance and her chest revealed. Thomas carried a pannikin of sugared tea to her and held it to her mouth as he had observed Bill doing previously, waiting while she sucked it back.

You ought to cover yourself up, missus, he said.

He gave her a share of his damper and he dipped some into the tea to soften for the child to eat. With his shirt sleeve he cleaned her face of dirt and ochre and she sat timidly while he did so, her child perched in her lap like some bald and doleful cat.

But the light showed them also the extent of the blood across that clearing; it was everywhere in a pattern that spoke of the chaos they'd wrought. As they ate, Batman and Black Bill studied the spatterings, each at times gesturing at places that the other had not seen. When they called Crook over to make sense of the trails, he offered his thoughts in his own tongue. He waved towards his legs, at the sky, at the bush. He laughed. He tugged at the fuzz on his chin.

Some dead he reckons, Pigeon said.

Crook nodded and gnawed on his damper.

What do you reckon? said Bill.

I reckon same.

Batman looked around at the blood trails. I want any dead found. I want em tallied. We'll see what we have bagged us.

. . .

The camp was sited in a clearing fired and shaped out of the rainforest over generations. It was tended land and the hand of the Plindermairhemener showed everywhere in its construction: in the narrows they'd shaped for coralling the kangaroo herds, in the island thickets that would hide their spearsmen, in the handholds hacked into the trees for possum hunting. Their blood lay upon the tended land now and the Vandemonian walked around those marks with his good boots crunching over the gum leaves, his eyes downcast.

It was in seeing his own boot prints run before him that he found reason to pause and look more closely. He knelt down. The earth was soft and his tread bold and well formed. He had crossed this way the night before and passed a man riddled with shot and holding his wounds. As he scanned the ground he saw where the blood crossed his prints and ran further off into the forest. Bill followed across the clearing and into the underscrub of wattle and fern. At the treeline he stopped and looked back at Batman and the Dharugs who were cocking their heads in study, but they did not see Bill enter the bush with his knife drawn.

He tracked through a shallow wooded gully at a trot and

every few yards he saw a stain or the scuffed earth of a heel print. Soon he snaked over a mossy scree that turned under his boots and the light was dim and misty. The clansfolk had split the crowns of every man fern in that glade for the edible shoot inside and the cut fronds hung like eyelids, brushing against his hat as he moved beneath. He stopped to look around, listening to the morning birds calling, turning his head to peer into the shadows. Nothing. He moved on.

Before long he arrived at a stone outcrop rising from the floor of the rainforest in great broken knuckles and he saw the marks in the mildew on those stones and knew he was close. A gully fell away below the outcrop and Bill stood atop those stones gazing down the embankment. Halfway down lay the clansman on his side where he had tumbled to a stop. The stones underneath were stained with his gore. Bill removed his hat and stood considering the descent.

Now the clansman turned his head to stare. Shot had flayed the skin from the forepart of his ribs and exposed the muscle and the pearly bone in parts. Above the wound he was ornamented in several places with scarring. Most of them were in the shape of halfmoons but along his shoulders he was scarred in neat rows and it was these scars that spoke of his clansmanship. Bill read those scars and saw that face and he understood: here was Taralta the lawman. The Vandemonian descended into that gully through the rank damp and he crouched beside Taralta. Even now mosquitoes covered the bare parts of him.

Bill brushed them off but Taralta had spent all night exposed and the flesh where they had fed was swollen and his thigh was embedded with scattershot and bruised in every shade of midnight. Such was his pain Taralta seemed barely to comprehend where he was. Bill raised him off the rocks.

They made a slow pace towards the campsite. The lawman was holding his wounds and leaning into Bill, smearing blood on Bill's shirt as they hobbled along. A short way off a tiger-wolf raised its head to observe them, its dog's eyes unblinking. Taralta looked at the creature but then turned away quickly as if he was ashamed to be seen in such a state.

Say now. What have you there? said Batman as they emerged into daylight.

Bill dropped the lawman where he fell. Lost in his pain, Taralta moaned and gritted his teeth. They poured water over his wounds which set him twitching and hollering. From a short distance away the girl called to him, clutching her child. Taralta took some ragged breaths and the girl in her bindings tried to edge near him but she was hauled off by Black Bill and dumped beside a bark hut.

They stood over Taralta in thought.

Wont see morning, said John Batman.

Gould was beside him. Well we have us one, he said. What of the others?

That there is a very fine question, said Batman.

...

All about that campsite roamed a plague of dogs like nothing they had ever put eyes on. Black Bill sucked on a gum leaf and studied the dusty swarm wheeling around, their diamond eyes coruscating in the firelight; each the same sort of wormridden thing built of bone, skin and bile. Some were engaged in licking blood off the bracken or the dirt and some nosed through the temma in the manner of pigs in a wallow, turning out the skins and the feather bundles lining the huts. The stink of them and their faeces was something utterly unholy. Bill removed the leaf from his bottom lip and turned to Batman.

Forty-eight, he said. Thirty of which is bitches.

Batman looked at him. A regular little herd, aint it.

Bill watched him.

They'll make havoc with me sheep.

No more needed to be said on the matter. Black Bill collected his weapon and he looped the strap across his shoulder and proceeded to wade out among the dogs. Glancing around at each other the assigned men watched him go, but they did not seem to understand his purpose so they leaned back against the blue gums and closed their eyes for some sleep. The dogs stood off from Bill and watched him as he drew alongside them. Making as if he held food he called a few to him and let them sniff his empty palm. Then he raised the fowling piece to his hip and fired into the head of an earthcoloured bitch.

A tremendous clap went up and the assigned men jumped at the sound. The dog spun a wild circle and folded upon itself.

It lay in a welter of blood, its head mostly removed. The pack had sprung off and now waited uneasily at a distance. As Bill repacked the barrel the little native child began to bawl.

The dogs dropped their ears. He approached close to a tall lean whippet and levelled the barrel near its neck. The fowler thundered and the dog burst in a bloody mess of fur and flesh as if detonated from the inside. The report cannoned along the mountainside away and away. Bill calmly repacked. The boy retrieved his weapon and came to lend his aid and they coralled more dogs into a confine between the temma where the animals huddled in fear. They both fired into that gathering and one fell plainly dead and another dragged itself through the dirt whining until it was brained with a stock.

The tang of sulfur and burnt hair hung upon the campsite. Batman looked at Baxter and at Gumm where they sat watching the grim spectacle with the ease of gents.

Well? said Batman.

Well what?

Get to it.

Baxter buttoned up his meagre coat and reached for his piece. This is niggers' work, he said under his breath.

Make sure you do the bitches especially, said Batman. He stood looking down at Jimmy Gumm but Gumm did not move. He was feeling the contusions on his head where the boy had taken to him.

You hopin to get yerself shot? said Batman.

Gumm lifted his eyes. No sir.

Batman drew his belt pistol and thumbed back the hammer. Take heed, he said.

Gumm scrambled to his feet.

By now a good few carcasses lay about on the dirt, and blood and bits of bone and innards covered the ground. The dying raised their heads out of that grime and cried and Pigeon walked among them brandishing a discarded waddy, bringing the club down across their snouts with such force that blood sprayed and rained down, staining his hat and shirt. They hauled the carcasses two at a time to the bonfires; their internals stringing out and steaming in the cold, gathering the leaf litter. Their hamcoloured tongues lolling from their mouths. Once alight the revolting smoke set the assignees gagging but they piled dogs up until the flames licked the boughs of the trees arching above. The washing of fire exposed jawbones and knuckled teeth and ribcages. The boy slapped his sticky hands against his trousers.

Black Bill looked him over. It's done.

The boy nodded. His shadow flickered in torn flaps of firelight. What do you think that means? he said.

He indicated the place where John Batman and Pigeon and Crook were gathered in discussion. Crook was gesturing down the mountainside at the primeval forest mantling the valley. On the ground beside him lay a freshly rolled firestick and Batman spat into his hands, rubbing them over before he picked it up. He blew into the embers and a little flame took hold which he pinched out to make a smoulder. He seemed to be preparing himself for another push into the backblocks.

Means more walking, said Bill.

I reckoned as much. The boy unbound his feet, shook the mud off the rags and set to retying them.

Bill walked over to join Batman and the Dharugs.

Down valley there you find some buggers, said Pigeon.

They'll be like fleas in bloody dog's fur down there, said Batman.

Bill surveyed the phantasmal hills beyond. We have the girl.

One young gin and one old storyteller dont justify what the Governor has outlaid on this. He wont pay us.

We need us some of the menfolk then, said Bill. Big ones.

The stouter the better. Meanlookin bastards.

Then it is settled.

Batman gazed at the forested slopes and replaced his hat. She's settled all right, he said. He lifted his firestick and signalled for Bill to follow.

The assigned men were standing before the blaze, pressing their sleeves to their faces as the acrid smoke of dog blew past. Great brumes of it like thunderheads brought to earth. Batman looked at them, man after man, and spoke.

Keep that there fire burning for a mark. Elsewise you'll be lost out here. Nothin but crows fer company. And be sure that gin can still walk when I get back.

The assigned men and the manservant William Gould shuffled about anxiously but voiced no objections to the plan as it was proposed. They scratched their groins and watched Batman resettle the doublebarrel gun on his back and move off.

He walked a few paces down the hill before something prompted him to stop and look around. You want a written tender? he said. On yer feet.

The Dharugs took up their effects and followed him.

The blood of men, women, dogs intermixed in a muddy wallow where the vanguard of four walked; they slipped and staggered across that killing field towards the forested valley, Batman cursing, the Dharugs less perturbed. The boy jumped up, following the men down the slope.

Hold on, he said, but the men continued and he hurried to catch them.

Stay, boy, said Bill. This is not for you.

No chance.

It will be dangerous.

I aint stupid like them back there. The blacks might come for their kin and then it will go to shite, wont it. Leave them to it I say.

You are learning, boy.

I am.

THEY WALKED DOWN THROUGH A DRY creek bed lined with swamp gums grown so close together they appeared as one living whole. The men passed around these trees in single file, among sun shafts which pierced the canopy but threw no light upon their faces nor warmed their bones. In the gloom the air was thick with flies and the mushrooms grew like the sightless larvae of some queer and unnamed vermin. Before long they found themselves among a stand of trees which had been stripped of their bark for windbreaks. The naked trunks were carved over with bisected circles, detailings of the moon and sun, images of snakes and roo. The Parramatta men gazed at the finely wrought icons but John Batman found more to hold his attention. Pressed onto the flesh of the tree was a bloody handprint. Batman removed his hat and crouched to examine the ground and Black Bill joined him. One injured man had passed this way.

They moved on. Somewhere south of Ben Lomond in a tomb of rainforest the trackers came to a stop before a vast easement and stood staring up, their hands atop their heads. They picked over the mossy stone for any trace of the clan, crouched and fingered the cragged surface for tailings of dirt or crushed grass or any sign that might suggest a direction taken, but found nothing. John Batman leaned on his gun and looked over that sorry landscape. He pulled out his quart flask of rum and threw a gill down his throat. By the time he had replaced it within the folds of his coat he was set upon a return to his own Kingston and the warm pleasures of his wife. He signalled the Dharugs down and led his group back into the bush.

That afternoon they retraced their track through the wilderness. Huge emergent gums broke the canopy and their uppermost foliage scraped the hulls of clouds dredging across the sky. But the sunless floor of that forest, kept shaded by acacia, sassafras and musk, was as wretched cold as the mountainside they had earlier quit. In time they left the trees and crossed a sequestered meadow where wallabies grazed. The animals watched the rovers advance before pounding away in unison, the sound like war drums beating inside the core of the earth. The men followed the slope of the mountain upwards and into the forest once more. Just beyond the fringe of trees the Vandemonian bent to one knee to study the ground.

There is a depression here, he said. Bill used his finger to outline a mark in the undergrowth. The wounded took rest in this place, he said.

Leaving the boy squatting in the bracken they circled around looking for a sign, fanning out to the points of the compass and scouring the groundcover. Bill soon found one trail of blood. He stepped with care through the little ferns where the red mottling glistened and he followed it to the base of a dead swamp gum, its trunk split apart. Balled up and wedged inside was a young warrior. Black Bill showed him the barrel. The warrior was stonyfaced and sweating. Each held the eyes of the other as Bill primed the cock of his gun.

I have him, he called.

They gathered at the hiding place.

You have a knack for this you do, said Batman.

The clansman had taken most of the scattershot in his thigh and some in the knee and when they tried to haul him upright he would not be moved but only called out in pain. He was written with scars, some the consequence of ritual, others of war, and there was a look of sombre contempt about his features as he clutched his shot knee and met their stares. Perhaps he saw some small victory in his resistance or sought to impede them anyhow. His leg bled sluggish and dark and he wiped his hands on the bracken.

Batman lifted off his hat, smoothed back the black hair beneath and replaced it. He looked down at the clansman before glancing away. Then he dropped his firestick and unslung his doublebarrel gun.

Yer ball, he said to Bill.

The Vandemonian uncinched a pouch from his belt and passed it to Batman and Batman stood the stock on the ground and held the gun by the mouth. An iron tamping rod was hidden in a channel between the barrels and he slid it free and placed it in his teeth. The barrels were octagonal in shape and the folds in the steel showed along the twin lengths like the grain in polished wood, irregular and organic. Etched into the sideplates were detailings of an eight-point stag surrounded by rosebushes and a nameplate bearing the Manton mark. Batman dosed the mouths from a powder horn and fed in a handful of grapeshot from Bill's pouch. He tamped that with the rod, then ripped off two little squares from a width of cotton kept for the purpose in his coat pocket and wadded them down behind the ball.

Batman considered the silent man secreted there in the hollow and thumbed back the hammers. He put one foot either side of the clansman's outstretched legs and showed him the long void of those bores, standing thus prepared through a few creakings of the trees. The warrior was wide-eyed, looking to Bill and to the Dharugs.

The eruption raised the birds squealing from the branches. As the gunsmoke cleared the fellow slumped forward and spilled upon the soil a stream of arterial blood. The hollow behind was peppered with pieces of skull and other matter. John Batman snapped open the locks, cleaned out the pans with his cloth and mopped the blood off the barrels. He looked around at the rovers.

The boy was openmouthed, pale, and he stared at the ruination laid out there at his feet and stepped back as the blood ran near his rags. The Dharugs had by now turned away and did not look back. They began retracing their track through the rainforest, picking among the fallen trunks. But Black Bill alone among that party met Batman's eye. He resettled his fowling piece across his back and spat on the ferns, watching Batman. Batman pulled out his rum, popped loose the cork, and drank. He held out the vessel to Bill. The Vandemonian looked at him. Then he turned to follow the Parramatta men out among the lemon myrtles and antique pines.

DARKNESS OVERTOOK THE COMPANY AS THEY emerged from the tree-line onto a hunting grassland where a flock of cockatoos grazed like yard fowl. They gathered firewood and beneath a bare and tumorous blue gum made a camp, for there was no light to travel by. John Batman struck a fire from the firestick he carried and tended the flames. They roasted the strips of mutton they'd each carried and watched the stars uncloak. All knew a wretched night awaited when the dew stiffened into frost and the grassland began to white over. They had no billycan as it was with the other men, so they boiled water in their mugs and held the handles through their sleeves. John Batman chose a coal from the fire and lit his pipe. He blew smoke out his nostrils before handing it on to the boy, who took his turn and let the flavour fill his mouth. He blew through his nose as Batman had and gave the pipe to Black Bill.

What do you spose happened to old Horsehead? said the boy.

John Batman was sitting cross-legged like a Chinaman with his hat on one knee. He looked away upcountry. Not my concern no more.

Will you track him?

We'll do better without his sorry bones about.

The night was bitter and all save John Batman wore their blankets around their shoulders. Batman was close to the fire and feeding it wood. Pigeon had his own pipe burning and with each draw the coal glow lit him; he smiled at mention of Horsehead.

Them Vandiemenland buggers cook him on fire and eat him I reckon. Eat him bones clean up.

He laughed and so did Crook.

They never eat men do they? asked the boy.

Couldnt say, said Batman.

What about them Parramattas?

Couldnt say.

Pigeon's havin a lend, aint he?

Batman stared at him. He slurped his tea. Couldnt say.

The boy studied the Dharugs and his face darkened. He drew his legs up tight, out of their reach. No, it werent the blacks, he said. He's just run off is all. He has designs on being a bushranger you know. A new Brady or some such.

That horsefucker aint worth a hair on Brady's arse, said Batman. He spat into the fire.

I heard told you yourself lagged the outlaw, said the boy, up Launceston way.

And that's the truth of it.

He must've bin a catch.

He was that.

Ow was it done?

How was it done, Batman murmured to himself. He held back the story as if he was reluctant but it was more likely an artifice of the telling, a telling he had honed over the many years since. He stoked the little fire. You dont take a man like Brady. More probably he relents. So it was with me.

Did you shoot him?

We had after him and we took a brace of guns but we never shot the man. There was some sharpshooters present too, I tell you. Fellows who could shoot the pizzle off a rutting buck if they so chose it. Men who knew guns like you know your own fingers or damn near.

The boy held his tin mug and the steam melted into the darkness around him. He watched Batman intently.

They was every breed of men, said Batman, but they shared a common enough trait and that was a fondness for money. The bounty stood at a hundred guineas you see. A sum intended to turn Brady's own gang upon him and set every man in the district at his heels. There's a good measure of cunning in our old Governor, a good measure. He reck-oned rightly that such a sum would stir the appetites of them what'd called Brady their man and stir them it did, lad. Now there was parties like the one I had formed tracking hither and thither after the man and his gang. He was doomed and every man alive knew it as a cold certainty that Brady would be hunted to a standstill, whereupon guns would be drawn and the death shot exchanged. What I intended was to be the man who fired it.

The boy watched him. But you never did, he said.

No I never. And more's the pity for that man. It was a herd of cows give him away in the end. The great man what near raised the island into revolution. Aye. There was these cows come rumbling down a field close to our camp. I know cows, and cows wont do aught without incentive and I watched em run and figured upon their havin cause to do so. So I took up arms and left camp to have me a little look-see.

You went alone?

I did. Foolish as it might sound now, I held no fear of Brady. Some believed that he was better than the common thuggery. Somethin grander. Some believed he was Irish gentry cast out for his politics. They believed a good many things about him and none of them true. But when I at last laid my young eyes on the wretched sight Brady had become, I was confirmed in my opinion of him as a brave man but doomed. For never would you see a more pitiable creature than what he presented. I came upon him at some distance limping across a paddock with the aid of a crutch. There was no army and nothing of the rebellion about him. Just a single beggarly figure straggling over a landscape nearly Irish in its greenery.

I almost broke off right there. Plenty of people since said I should have. John Wedge allowed that he was the nearest we'd ever have to a Red MacGregor and as such deserved his peace. But I couldnt come at that when I was younger. I supposed a man should suffer for his sins. Even a great man. There was also the matter of a hundred guineas weighing on me thinking. I am since changed in my opinions though. I followed him onwards and he staggered into a bit of bush and after a time I crossed the field in pursuit and it wasnt far till I caught him. Holed up snug under a bush he was. Muddier than a miner. I showed my gun and he raised his likewise.

By now a deep cold had come down and the stars gleamed like minerals. Batman gazed up at the sky a moment to study those brilliant stones before he continued.

I held my firearm and I looked him dead in the eye. We stood off a good minute. Then Brady asks me who the hell I was. And I says John Batman at your service. He is in pain somethin terrible. He asks if I'm a military man. I says to him, I'm not a soldier—now surrender for there is no chance for you.

Batman swirled the dregs of tea then drained them on the grass and slipped the mug into his pocket. But I know this much. I ought to have shot the bastard. When he was dropped his neck held they say. He danced on the gibbet like he was back a-courting in County Kildare. There aint a man in history who deserves to die like that. I ought to have shot him and had done with it.

The judges, the parsonry, the public servants, they never get their hands dirty with men's blood and they are the worse for it. There is a sly cruelty to a fellow who sends others to their death while he himself has no knowledge of it. But I'd say one minute beside a dying man with all his flailing and begging would set their thinking to rights.

The boy shivered inside his blanket. Brady had it coming, he said.

Batman leaned in and the underside of his jaw was lit up ghoulishly by the fire. We all of us have it coming, lad.

Bits of mutton in the flames smoked in a dark crescent. The boy watched him still. What about that witch? Does he?

The witch, said Batman. He nodded slowly.

Does he?

I will tell you somethin about him. There isnt a particle of manhood about that savage. Not more than a speck. His weapons of choice are a treachery patiently nursed and some knowledge of hides and snugs. He deserves a dog's death and by God he will get it.

After the talking was done Black Bill rose, tea in hand, and melted into the night to relieve himself on the bushes. When he returned the men had lain down for sleep and Bill did likewise, but not before building the fire up against the weather. Only the boy remained awake. He watched Bill settle once more and drag his blanket around his shoulders. The flames twitched and danced between them.

We aint runnin foul of the law ourselves are we? said the boy. I mean, Batman up and shot that black bugger.

Black Bill tugged his hat down over his eyes. He eased back against the meat of the blue gum. You cant murder a black, he said, any more than you can murder a cat.

The boy drew breath to speak but in the end had nothing more to say. The fire popped, the only sound to mar the limitless dark. He pressed two fingers against his cheek and brought them to his mouth and licked and remembered the taste of apples.

THE SUN THREW A WEAK LIGHT around the mountain and John Batman walked the perimeter of their little camp looking upcountry for smoke from the signal fire. The frost rasped under his boots as he strode, leaving prints the colour of grass. The sharings of damper were miserly small and they ate quickly. They pissed on the fire and then Batman led them over the plain where feet both booted and bare grew numb as their progress was written upon the hoarfrost. They retraced their own run through the forest and up the slope where the going was steepest and all that morning the sun was merely a rumour in the sky. By afternoon it revolved around the mountainside and shone upon the backs of the company. At a stream they lay in the slick litter and drank and refilled their canteens and Pigeon indicated a gap in the canopy where smoke as thin as a feather floated against the blue day and marked the locality of the assigned men. They pressed on, taking a bearing through the brush that gave easier passage, and the miles ran by.

Within a few hours they had found the camp. The assignees and Gould seated around the signal fire stood and brought their weapons up. They looked badly done with, dark under the eyes and unwashed. Jimmy Gumm had the native boy on his hip and he approached the group with the little boy clinging to his shirt and sucking his wet finger. Baxter and Gould looked upon John Batman with much the same satisfaction, as they'd supposed the company murdered and themselves lost on the mountain. They grinned and walked towards him. The child's mother was roped beside the fire and Taralta lay nearby, his eyes closed, his breath shallow. They had wrapped his wounds and fed him although quite why they could not say.

Some sort of sled's what's needed, said Gumm. To drag him on.

Batman didn't respond. Instead he walked away from the fire and waved at his men to follow him. They formed up in a rough curve, those bleakfaced men, and stood with their arms folded on their chests. Batman looked them each in the eye as if he was no part of that group but was indeed its opposition. His massive gun was longwise on his back, the leather strap and buckle on his chest in the manner of a military crossbelt, and he unslung that fearsome piece and held it out before him. The men waited in silence.

Who will it be then?

They glanced at one another.

The child was wailing, a thin, carrying sound. John Batman held his weapon. They shifted under his burdensome gaze and scratched their balls until he raised his voice again.

I aint doin it, he said.

But no one stepped forward. They made a study of the ground and would not raise their eyes.

And so it was that Black Bill grabbed the doublebarrel gun from Batman's hand and he checked the priming and walked off towards the campfire. They watched him go and they one and all shook their heads. Batman called them onwards with a motion of the arm, so they hefted their hide knapsacks and affixed their weapons across their backs and then they followed him. Someone lifted the native girl to her feet and shoved her along and her child rode on Gumm's broad and lashscarred shoulders. Soon they were gone altogether. Black Bill removed his hat. He worked back the heavy cocks of both barrels and they settled with a dull clunk. Taralta clutched at his swaddled chest and looked Bill in the eyes, as wordless as ground stone. Bill brought up the massive gun and steadied the barrels across his forearm as his broken fingers could not take the weight. The sight of those octagonal bores levelled on him caused the lawman to huddle down behind his hands and cry out, and Bill steadied the gun but there was no clear shot he might take. He waited.

See now, he said. Move your hands.

The lawman crabbed away over the dirt, still with his arms

upraised, and Bill followed him and kicked him in the bandaged ribs and kicked at his arms.

menenger, Bill said, menenger.

The lawman curled up more tightly. Bill brought the heel of his boot to bear on the wounded man but he kicked in vain while Taralta folded his arms ever tighter around his head.

Black Bill lowered the gun. Wattlebirds made their yac-a-yac coughs in the bush behind and he gazed at the blue hills to the south and the snow clouds forming above them. When Bill looked again at the lawman he was watching through his hands, dirt and ash stuck in the cords of his ochred hair. Bill brought the gun up, balanced it across his arm again and tucked the butt into his shoulder. Then he fired into the lawman's head.

The almighty concussion rattled the wind in his chest and the gun bucked from his grip and fell. He turned away, holding his shoulder. Blood had spattered his face, his arms, the front of his shirt. For a time he would not look at the body of the lawman where it lay near the fire. He rubbed at the bruising on his shoulder; watched storms amass around the southern peaks. After a while he turned to survey the slaughter he had wrought.

One of the lawman's arms was gone at the elbow and the teeth seated in the jawbone could be seen through the cheek. There was flesh blown every place. He picked up the Manton gun. The locks were soiled and he fingered out the grime, and then with the corner of his coat cleaned the pan and blew into the latchworks. He brought the weapon up to eye level and peered along its sights for barrel warps or any misalignment then, content, slung the leather on his shoulder. Without a rearward glance he stalked off, his hat replaced, his boots slipping in the blood. Smoke from the fire blew around him in a snarl raised on the wind and dispersed again on the same.

...

Black Bill made haste after the roving party. He pushed onwards through clumps of tree ferns and followed the track taken by the company down the mountainside. They were no more than ten minutes ahead but he had neither sight nor sound of them. He paused to study the scuffings of bandaged feet and the direction they told before moving on.

He was picking a careful path down an embankment strewn with debris when he heard it. He stopped and looked back at the mountain rising behind him and the silver snow it wore crownlike. The bush of black wattle and blossoming gum was broken only by the path he was scouting. He brought Batman's gun around. Off in the forest the crashing of some nameless thing sounded, at first indistinct but ever less so. It may have been wallaby or emu but as he listened, as he made that din for what it was, he was gripped in a moment of panic.

He bolted down the slope, finding a position in the

undergrowth where he might hide, and he tugged the branches around himself and cast up the debris of the forest floor across his legs to obscure his clothing. In that blind he allowed himself only the smallest gap to see up the hillside as he settled the gun under his chin and concealed it too with leaves. He slowed his breathing, stilling every movement of his limbs. By the time he was embedded, the dark shapes of spearsmen were beginning to show among the yellow gums that stood mute and immovable as the men streamed around them. They dipped behind a fallen tree and vaulted its trunk and their great spears rose tall overhead. Black Bill had them along his barrel as his heart beat a lively rhythm against the earth but he held off taking his shot. They were driving before them a familiar figure, a baldheaded fellow crazed with horror, glancing behind and clawing his way through the underscrub. The warriors made war cries and hammered their waddies against the trees, setting the branches a-shudder and sending their spears sibilating between the gums. Bill watched one haft arc and bury in the earth beside Horsehead, who went down on one knee but rose and fought onwards towards the spot where Bill was concealed. Among the war party was Manalargena. He waved his blackwood waddy above his head and the clay caking in his beard shook as he hurtled through the forest. He was painted up for war in grey ash and red ochre. Behind him the terrible tribe howled in one voice as they followed their quarry.

In those few seconds Black Bill considered letting the

clansmen simply pass by. He was well hidden. No good would come of helping Horsehead. But the old crook was nearly spent and he loped along with the gait of a river troll, his wispy hair awry above his haggard face, his clothes torn and grime on his skin. As Bill watched, a ten-foot spear buried half its length into a tree fern just shy of Horsehead and he cried out to God for help. Instead the task fell upon Bill. He cursed himself for a fool. Then he rose out of the brush bearing the gun on his hip and fired into the war party. Immediately they dropped and one screamed out in pain and they scrambled a retreat up the hillside, keeping low behind the gums and leaving the distressed fellow where he lay. Only Manalargena remained standing and he did not turn or hide but rather he stared across that separation of forest at the Vandemonian. He raised aloft his waddy and called out, nina krakapaka laykara.

The Vandemonian might have fired the second barrel but he would have left himself exposed without a charge. The headman hooted and wailed.

Shoot the bastards. Horsehead was crouched behind a broken stump. Shoot shoot shoot, he said.

But Black Bill had gone running into the scrub hunched over and Horsehead now bolted after him, stumbled and righted himself, and they put in some yards before the Plindermairhemener lobbed their waddies end over end through the trees. Those cudgels whoomping in slow rotations battered the gums overhead and gouged out huge wounds in the hardwood. There was more cover down the slope, thickets of heath, of flowering musk, and as they struck out towards it the headman's cries drowned in the clamour of wind.

...

They fought them running down the face of the mountain all that long day. They found cover behind crowds of ferns and mossy rocks while Bill repacked and fired at the noiseless black shapes flitting between various concealments. Noon saw them stop at a water trickle and they took turns lapping at the stones as the other kept watch. Bill refilled his canteen. Then they moved on once more but that small halt gave the clansmen back some ground and they quickly drew within range of a good throw. A spear curved over Bill's hat and fell without a sound in front of him, the haft quivering in the earth. He frowned and broke the thing over his knee but more followed the first and soon the trees were full of their clatter. He picked up his pace and Horsehead stayed with him. The Plindermairhemener retrieved their spears as they ran and threw them again and they neither spoke nor cried out but maintained the silence of hunters.

In the afternoon the two marked men crouched amid the ruins of a dried river bed and studied the clansmen where they held positions up the slope in the dogwood. Black Bill opened the neck of his shot bag and felt at the contents. Perhaps ball enough for one barrel. He retied the string and stuffed the sack inside his drum then looked around at Horsehead.

You hear that? he said.

The old cur nodded. I hear it. He jibbered the same stuff at me all night.

Manalargena was calling to Bill across the distance between the parties. He called him plague dog and speculated on the nature of the white sickness Bill had so plainly contracted. He insisted that Bill would be killed as mercifully as any diseased animal if he came forth in surrender and would not suffer the punitive rituals of spearing or wounding reserved for transgressors of the law. Bill listened and waited and when the headman had finished his oratory he stood from the cover and fired. The men dropped away before the spout of flame. All except the headman. Bill stood with the gun against his shoulder assessing the position he held and then he went low and fast through the brush and Horsehead went after him. They ran for where the black wattle grew broad and would shelter them from sight as the clansmen renewed their cries of war.

THE ROVING PARTY HAD SETTLED ON a piece of rocky mountainside cut across by southerlies as cold as glass, and lit only by the halfmoon affixed above the hills silhouetted in the west. They sat in that subterranean darkness, wrapped in their blankets, with their pieces in hand as they chewed on raw mutton strips. Gunfire had sounded all day along the mountain's flanks and from fear of an ambush they had made no fire as the night drew down. Pigeon would not take his ease and he strode the edge of the rocks in silent observation, awaiting some sign of the Plindermairhemener. They had fashioned a rope collar for the girl and tied her hands at her back that she might be more easily led and she lay in her skins staring from her one unswollen eye at the Dharug man as he moved back and forth. Her child sat near her, shapeless in the dark but for his white eyes.

No feature could be told out of that shrouded forest save what shadows were thrown up by the moon and John Batman tossed a small stone at Pigeon and motioned for him to quit.

He looked at Batman, drew his blanket around his shoulders and moved off again at his scouting. And despite the savage cold most of them found sleep in whatever positions they held, beside and leaned against one another, and still Pigeon walked the boundary. He had slept not a shade the previous night and would not this night. It was near midnight when a call of cooee cut the silence. Pigeon nudged his countryman Crook and bade him to rise. Batman had chucked off his covers, finding his weapon even before the call had died on the air. The scrub beneath their outlook was a formless black and silver gradient along the mountain's flanks, and they studied that sweep of country for what little they could make of it. Again came the call and the men in one motion aimed their weapons at the quarter from which it had emanated. John Batman was wary of this ploy and he would not return the cooee as was customary along the frontier. He walked out a short way and stood listening above the insect din. When the call sounded a third time it was followed by some words he could not make out. He turned to Pigeon.

What do you spose that was?

Pigeon grinned. Said he found some old cretin.

Who said?

Our Billy Black.

Batman kicked at the ground. Did he? Well call him in then.

Through his hands Pigeon bellowed out his own cooee and it was returned a moment later. The men stood down, eased back the hammers of their pieces, and before too long the stragglers approached the campsite and wordlessly sat themselves down among the others. Horsehead had fared poorly and was shivering and bleeding. He set his grubby feet upon the stones, and by the moon's light plucked thorns and tended the various gashes in his soles.

We believed you lost, said Jimmy Gumm.

I was, said Horsehead. Now I'm found.

He worked with great tenderness upon a two-inch score in his foot, probing it for remnants of splinter. I had a time of it with the crows, but.

Where's yer piece? said Batman.

Out bush somewheres.

Christ almighty.

Horsehead sipped a mouthful of water and spat into the gash. The pain had him wincing. You see em too, Bill?

I did. They were tracking Mr. Clarke here.

And near had me too, by God.

They mean to raise Cain I reckon, said Batman. We'd do well to watch our backs.

I saw that chief atheirs, said Horsehead.

Ugly heathen wretch, aint he? said Batman.

I had no weapon or I would've bagged him meself. Bill there, he shot up a pound-weight of ball and I seen him drop one at least. But not that chief. No. He has some cunning in him, he does.

We havent the wherewithal to take him. He is beyond us.

They all looked around at Bill. He said nothing more but merely pushed back the brim of his hat and brought his features into the moonlight and they watched him proceed to pick at the dry scabby cakes of blood spattered up his arms, the blood of dogs, of clansmen, and some of his own.

AT NOON THE FOLLOWING DAY THE bush first thinned over a few yards then evaporated entirely as the party approached the open grounds of Kingston. A change of temper washed over them and talk rounded to rewards and their spending, rum and its swilling, women and their laying. They retraced the curve of the field long ago burned from the forest by the Plindermairhemener. They passed the sheep bones and skerricks of yellowed wool that littered the ground, evidence of the slaughter committed upon Batman's flocks some years back by those same folk. They led the native girl along and her dull eyes saw but did not see. Her feet kicked over the bones that rattled like ruined pottery.

As they neared the farmhouse Batman's three girls came bolting over the paddocks and topping fences to embrace their father. The eldest stood back when she caught smell of his clothes but the little ones seemed untroubled and latched on around his legs.

Is she sick, Father? said the eldest. She was pointing at the black girl who'd dropped to her knees.

She aint no concern ayours. He hauled the girls off his legs and steered them towards their sister. For a moment the three girls lingered, their dresses catching on the breeze. Then the youngest spotted the child Jimmy Gumm had on his hip.

A baby. He has a baby, she said.

Get inside. Get! Batman yelled and the girls took off.

On Batman's word, Gould led the native girl to the outbuildings. The key groaned in the padlock as Gould cranked it around and the chains fell free from the looped handles of the store shed. He freed the crossbrace and yanked on the door and its toe scarred the earth as it moved. The faded afternoon sun issued through the separations in the woodwork and caught in the cobwebs. That was all the light the girl would have. Gould pushed her into the stink of wool and sheep shit, and shouldered the door shut. Not a sound did she utter.

. . .

When Eliza Batman appeared on the verandah she had in her hands a pisspot turned from wattle wood that contained their night's purgations and her girls were leading her along by the skirts, pointing at the party men as they neared the farmhouse—the boy in his clothes stiffened with dog's blood and the smiling black men and among them Jimmy Gumm holding the hand of a native child. Batman kept his distance until she'd slung the contents of the pisspot on the grass. She was a slight Irish woman, pockmarked but handsome still, and she met those men with a glare which made plain her displeasure.

And what by Jaysus is this?

A boy, mam.

She swung about on John Batman. A boy. So where's his mother?

Locked up.

Dont let's be lyin to each other, Johnny.

I aint lyin. She's locked there in that store shed.

In there?

That's what I said, woman.

She cut through those squalid bushmen with her three girls behind her and banged on the door of the store shed. She called out but there was no sound from inside. Open it, she said.

William Gould produced a ring of iron keys and from that selected one, shaking it free of the rest. He tugged the heavy door open in fits and starts. Eliza bent her head inside.

Fearsome little colleen that, said Gumm, but he was met by the stone cold eyes of John Batman and the grin he wore vanished. The native girl stumbled drunkenly into the noon glare. Immediately the child by Gumm's side began to keen for its mother.

Take care, said Gould. She has a set of claws on her.

But Eliza showed no caution as she stood taking summary of the girl from head to toe. The remnants of her ritual painting remained on her yet and the smeared ochre and white clay told of her providence among the people of the hills. The animal pelt she wore across one shoulder was crawling with fleas and stank of the smoke and grease of bushlife. She swayed under the baffling sun and covered her eyes with her roped hands.

Eliza looked around at the men. She's nothin but a child.

Batman grimaced. I dont care what she is.

Aye, she said. God's mill may grind slowly, John, but it grinds finely. You wont be forgot when he tallies what's owin.

...

Carrying the bucket between them Batman's girls ferried water from the creek and tempered it with boiled water from the kitchen, singing a hymn as they toiled. A small tin bath was borne from the house and stood on the verandah and the girl and her child were hitched to an upright beside it.

Dont be frettin now, missus, said Eliza.

Eliza hiked up her sleeves and leaned in to unfasten the knot around the native girl's neck. The coarse hemp had chewed at her skin and the girl flinched but did not resist. John Batman was backed against a fencepost, watching the spectacle from a gentlemanly remove with his gun held in the crook of his arm. Eliza steered the girl by the elbow towards the bathtub. Steam rose off the iron face of the water and the native girl hesitated at the edge.

Look, it wont hurt yer none. See? Eliza splashed water onto her dark skin. The girl put one foot into the water as Eliza tugged on her elbow, and then a tentative second. There she waited with her bound hands at her chest.

She wouldnt never have seen hot water before, said Batman.

Course she has. They love a mug of tea.

Dont bathe in it but, do they?

Go on with yer now. Barely sixteen she is. This aint no business ayours.

It'll be my business if she bites yer ear off, wont it?

Go on!

Batman crossed his weapon behind his neck and walked off.

Eliza lifted the child also into the water and he thrust out his squat legs and churned up the surface. Using a cookpot she ladled water over the girl's shoulders. It ran and beaded over the grease on her skin. So she took a block of soap and raised a lather over the whole of her back and thighs and arms and all the while the girl stood meekly and fixed her eyes downwards.

Here, Maria. You do it. Eliza gave the pot to her eldest and the girl rolled up the sleeves of her pinny and knelt beside the bath.

Look here at these scars on her.

Dont be touchin them now.

What's her name?

Goodness only knows.

I should like to call her Ellen. Could I call her Ellen, Ma?

Eliza straightened up, her backbones cracking. Katherine, she said. Come up here, would you?

Bill's woman was belting wet clothes against a stone and upon hearing her name she lifted her head. Her long hair was tied back like a white woman's and her head came up slowly as if that coil was a great weight to bear. Eliza waved her nearer and she came, wiping her hands on the tattered men's shirt she wore loosely over her belly.

What's her name?

Eh?

I want to know her name.

Her?

Yes.

She no one.

She has a name, dont she?

Katherine looked the girl over. Why you want that?

Well fer goodness sake, I must have something to call her.

You call her anythin.

Just be askin after her name, wont yer, please.

So Katherine turned to the girl. mullarwalter nela? she said. But the girl was mute. She brought her face down level and stared into the girl's eyes. mullarwalter nela? she said again. nina tunapri mina kani?

Luggenemenener.

Luggenemenener?

narapa. The girl didn't look up.

The water was a rich soup of oil and scum. Maria dumped a potful on the child's head and scrubbed his hair and she likewise rubbed the girl's shaven head and her cicatricial skin where inset circles of sun and moon moved below her flesh like the burrowed grubs of moths. The soap picked out those scars and outlined them as they had been previously outlined by clay.

No name, Katherine said as she wiped her hands on her shirt.

She must have a name. Even dogs have names.

But Katherine's mouth had turned hard and a moment passed where it seemed she might walk off. Whites got no need of our name, she said. You call us anythin.

Having spoken her piece she stepped off the verandah and resumed her washing, the steady slap tolling endlessly across the flats. Eliza pressed her no further. They pulled the girl from the bathtub and unbound her hands and yanked a worn dress over her head. It sagged off her thin limbs, looking no more proper on her than it would have on a gum sapling. They did up her child in an old pinny and in the afternoon sun the two made a morose pair, gazing down at their clothes. Eliza bundled the kangaroo pelt onto the kitchen fire and pointed at the flames taking hold and at the rich greasy smoke they shed.

You dont need it no more, she said to the native girl. Dont need it. You have a good dress now.

And they all stood watching the rainbow forktongues lick along the outers and singe away the fur in a stink of char.

THE ASSIGNEES WERE POSITIONED AROUND A stewpot gurgling on the fire and one by one William Gould dipped their bowls into the mess of meat and dumplings. The stew steamed as they shovelled with spoons carved from sheep's ribs. As they ate those five faces remained fixed upon John Batman. He was heading across from the store shed and he had on his shoulder a firkin of rum which he eased down among the assignees. He produced a wooden bungstarter and tapped it open and the earthy black liquid inside fumed as he breathed deeply of it.

Horsehead chewed his mutton gristle. Seems Mr. Batman here means to do us a good turn, he said.

Fill your mugs and that'll do.

I'm partial to a good turn. Specially one what involves a finger or two of Indian.

I always reward obedience when I sees it, Clarke. To have such simple minds toiling away at my own bidding is the highest good.

The men filed past the little barrel and plunged their pannikins in and brought them out dripping.

Might I temper it with a dash of water? Gould said. Only me guts take poorly to rum, you see.

I dont much care if you suck it through your ringhole, Gould. But there'll be no singing and no rowdiness. I got three littluns asleep up there. I got a baby. None of it, you hear me?

At mention of the girls there came a whispering between the men. Who it was, what was said, was lost the moment Batman turned around. But as he met those eyes and the wattle bark of their weathered faces they smirked and looked about. He hammered the firkin closed. Shouldered it. He carried it as far as the campsite the blacks had made themselves before setting it down. The Parramatta men sucked on the last of their meat while John Batman tapped open the casket and filled their mugs as well. Pigeon tossed bones on the fire and wiped his hands on his stringy hair. He raised to his lips the mug of rum and drew on it.

You wake me. Anything happens. Batman pointed at them with the mallet.

Crook grinned. He held up his mug.

I watch em, said Pigeon. Old man Crook, he bloody sleep I reckon.

Batman stood there in the firelight gazing down at the assignees, grouped there in the shade of the moon and the fire's fluid light. Then he carried the firkin back to the farmhouse.

. . .

Bill and his woman crossed the paddocks under an icecoloured moon, surrounded by ewes aglow in the moon sheen. Broad and unshorn, the ewes stared like imbeciles as the pair topped the chock and log and continued on their way, the mud sucking at his boots, at Katherine's bare feet. They pushed on to where the forest rose sheer from the earth in a gloom of pillars and they told direction by the moon while hundreds of feet overhead the possums squabbled for territory. In good time they came to the clearing, cut and burned from the bush, and to the bark humpy they'd raised together in readying for the birth of their son. They moved between the grey stumps and the halfcut saw logs. Bill dragged the door open, still holding his wife's hand. Once inside she knelt at the hearth and kindled a meagre fire of sticks and dry gum leaves. As the flames grew she unlaced the boots from Bill's feet and set them beside the fire to dry. They ate cold stew without bread and drank their share of Batman's rum in hot sugared water and the firelight cast shadows up behind them on the wall, caricatures of those dark and soundless shapes slumped before the flames.

. . .

Gould yanked back his blanket. Pigeon at first continued to sleep, lost deep in liquor as he was, and he heard nothing of what was yelled. So Gould shook him and again called his name and Pigeon stirred and suddenly was awake.

The girl, he said haltingly. They want the girl.

Pigeon could hear raised voices and the ringing of metal in the distance. He stood up to better make out these goings-on.

You'll help, wont you? said Gould.

But Pigeon was already gone up the slope towards the store shed.

The assignees had an axe from somewhere. One of their number swung it against the door, burying it into the palings. Then he staggered back among his fellows, who caught hold of his arms and righted him, and he shook them off as if they were so many maidservants fussing about his person. He had tugged the axe handle free of the woodwork and come about to take a fresh swing at the door when Pigeon called out, Hey you buggers.

They all turned to face him. It was Horsehead gripping the axe and he jabbed the head at Pigeon. He was unsteady on his feet as the axe head waved before him.

Here, he said, you have a go, darkie. Horsehead made to pass the handle across to him.

Piss off you buggers piss off.

Swaying like sailors, the men watched him. Horsehead laughed. He seemed about to say something to the others and his mouth parted, but before a word was unloosed a weapon fired somewhere off in the night. Horsehead clutched his chest and doubled over, crying out, and sat down on the dirt. Gumm and Baxter and the boy broke towards the darkness of the fields. Pigeon watched them, unsure precisely what had taken place. He scratched at his chin and looked around. Standing shadowed before the faint light from the farmhouse was John Batman. Pigeon stepped promptly aside as he approached and Batman slid the packing rod out of his fowler, tamped down a fresh wad and raised the gun up to his eye.

I'm shot, said Horsehead and tried to stand up.

But Batman was over him and he discharged squarely between his shoulderblades. The miscreant crumpled headlong onto the mud. The others were bolting out across the fields in the blackness and Batman unstoppered his powder horn with his teeth, dosed up the weapon and squinted into the night.

You see em out there anywheres? he said around the cork.

But Pigeon was staring down at Horsehead where he lay groaning and twisting on the ground like a man gripped by a palsy and did not answer.

You see em or not? Batman said again.

This fella got no blood on him.

Acourse not.

Horsehead rolled over. I'm bloody shot, he moaned.

From his shirt pocket Batman pulled a handful of ball and fed it down the muzzle. That's one there, he said.

He took a few strides into the night then fired. The flash bloom lit the field and Jimmy Gumm was seen in that frieze shambling across the grass, his face stamped with the blood-fear that had seized hold of him.

Yelled Batman: What did I tell you bastards?

We never touched her, we never, I swear.

Come here where I can see you.

Darnt shoot, please darnt shoot.

Come here.

Murder, murder!

By Christ there'll be more than that.

A torrid wind blew up the valley and snatched at the smoke coiling from Batman's piece. He listened to the shrieks swirling, then turned on his heel and started back towards the farmhouse where Eliza watched from the verandah, shawled in a blanket, holding aloft a candle lamp. As he passed Pigeon he handed the gun over to him and strung the powder horn around his neck. He fished more of the ball out of his shirt and placed it in Pigeon's open palm.

Givem a bit more if you fancy it.

Pigeon looked down at the little dried pepperberries which Batman had been shooting. Pitted, hard and aromatic, the sort used often enough in stews or bakes. When he looked up Batman was already disappearing inside the doorway and the windows dimmed as he carried the light into the bedroom.

HARD UPON FIVE IN THE MORNING John Batman emerged onto the verandah, in his hands a mug of tea. He gazed out across the pale frosted expanse of paddock to the mountain beyond. Gould had risen early too. He had taken out the mare and harnessed her to the cart and they stood together, beast and man, while he fed her oats from his pocket and whispered in her twitching ear. Batman sipped his tea and waited for the sun to fully show itself. Then he set down his mug, stepped off the verandah and walked across the frost to the store shed to unlock the door. He put his head into the darkness. Nothing, no movement. So he vanished inside. Roosters called out for the dawn somewhere across the way in long strangled howls. When he reappeared he was hauling the black girl over the dirt by her ankle.

He stood looking down upon her and soon Gould joined him. She squinted into the sun rising above the horizon, her eyes a pair of the darkest marbles inlaid under her smooth wide forehead. She watched them but if she understood her fate she made no sign of it. The child blundered forth out of the shed and into the keen winter air and clutched its mother. John Batman caught it up by the straps of the pinny it was dressed in and slung it across his shoulder. The girl grunted at her bindings. As he paced back to the farmhouse she began to call. It might have been the child's name or it might have been cries for her own calamitous misfortune but they were words Batman had never heard spoken before that moment. Heedless, he carried her child inside the farmhouse and was gone.

The girl arched her back and her throat drew taut as she screamed. The hunting dogs roped at the farmhouse were set off baying along with her. She screamed until Gould struck her cleanly across the jaw. Blood ran from her lips where one of her teeth had come clean through the skin. She moved her head around to look up so he hit her again then stood back rubbing his bruised hand. The girl made no more sound after that. Her head lolled as he dragged her to the cart and dumped her onto the flatbed. The full risen sun spread gold streams around the cloud banks and over the roof of the scrublands; it cast light on one half of the girl's broken face but left the other melded in shadows. Gould's knuckle ached and he felt the joint, the sharp pain that followed meaning it was likely fractured. He kicked at the cold wet earth in frustration. There was nothing to be done for it so he climbed the bench and called the horse onwards along the road that led to Campbell Town and the lockup where she would be delivered.

...

Late in the afternoon of the roving party's third day at Kingston Gould returned. He jockeyed the cart over the shallow rise at a canter with the wheels raising arcs of mud and the hoofbeat like regimental drumming. Barely had the cart stopped before he dismounted and left the lathered horse steaming in the air. He climbed the verandah and hammered on the farmhouse door. It was swung to by a girl whose hair was bundled up in a ribbon as vivid green as the forest.

I've urgent need of your father. Is he inside?

The girl shook her head and pointed away over the brown pastures to a fire front burning slowly across it. Down there.

Inside, a haze deepened and filled out the shadows where Eliza sat with a pipe in her fingers and her feet propped on a deepbacked lambing chair. You find that big blathering skite, William, you tell him he haster come feed this boy. I'll be damned if I'm fer doin it.

A black child appeared next to the girl and brought his face up to study Gould, a face curved and smoothed like his mother's.

Da's callin him Ben, said the girl. She shoved him. The boy tumbled over and lay sprawled until he found his bearings and then he was up and about, none the worse for it. So the green-ribboned girl shoved him again and knocked him flat. But even that seemed not to upset him. He went off about whatever business he had among those Christians, away towards some darker corner of the room. Eliza chuffed on her pipe and paid him no mind as the smoke veiled her features.

...

Black Bill and the Dharugs walked behind the burn as it smoked across the pasture, roused along by the breeze. The damp kerchiefs bound over their faces were blackened about the mouth holes and lent them the look of bushrangers. Where the flames sputtered they touched off the dry grass again with the long brands they carried for the purpose and the flame fizzed through the bracken and saplings. All manner of thing came equally under that heat, the native fowl and badgers, the lizards. A snake still a-smoulder twisted among the blackened smoking grass where the men walked barefoot. They had burned from the leeward edge in the tribal manner, and those lanky men appeared as they must have on the endless never-never of their birth country, steeped in smoke and song and common purpose, remaking the place to their ends. On the windward side the assignees were ranged along the hard forest border and as the fire neared they beat the flames with boughs of green gum leaves so that the wooded belts between the fields might be preserved. They brought the boughs overhead then down and cinders rose and died on spectral updrafts. Soon they were dusted grey with ash.

John Batman stood by, sucking on a bottle of rum and water and admiring the violence of the burn as the smoke blanked out the sun. Behind the fire front the field lay charred and a shape came looming through the cloud. Batman rubbed the tears from his eyes and removed the handkerchief covering his mouth. It was Gould, dashing closer on his awkward bandy legs. He ran until he was in shouting distance. The heat had him sweating in runnels down his shirt. He leaned on his knees and heaved.

What is it has you bolting like a whipped whore?

More of em sighted, Gould said. Down Swanport way. A hundred or more I'm told.

John Batman squinted through the wash of smoke. Who says this then?

By now Gould had gone down on his haunches and he loosened his collar, breathing hard. He waved a soggy crinkled twist of paper at Batman.

Batman unfurled it and read. Then he raised his head. You brought back rations?

I did. What the sergeant would allow us at least. By which I should say not very much.

Shoes?

A half dozen pair.

Batman stood with the letter, looking out over the paddocks at the strange dark sky above them. A hawk turned against it, watching for little life fleeing the blaze. Batman stuffed the letter in his pocket and slowly tugged down the brim of his hat as if to shield his face from that huge sightless eye blazing overhead. He whistled to the men and signalled them in.

Pigeon and Crook and the Vandemonian gathered up and moved in, their shadows pulling over the charred grass. Batman passed his water flagon on and told them to drink and in turns the men swigged and returned the flagon when they were done. Soon the assignees gathered up as well and they drank and squatted in the cinders. Ash had darkened their clothes and stained their faces and they seemed all of one anonymous hue.

Weather's likely going bad, said Bill.

That it is, said Batman.

So we havent time to stand about, said Gumm. We need to get it done.

You have time fer this.

For what? said Horsehead.

Batman looked from man to man. Seems we have to do the needful once more, boys.

They nodded solemnly.

Out Swanport way. A hundred or more I'm told.

Black Bill pressed his hands to his hips. That's rough country.

Bloody Swanport, said Horsehead.

At that point Batman stepped towards the men and he sized them up each and every. She's a good eighty mile off, he said. Eighty mile of murder. But I tell you, we get them live heads and you get yer tickets. Plain and simple.

They would not meet his gaze.

He shook his head in disgust, turned to the Dharug men. What say you, Pigeon?

The tracker scratched his balls. We. Us nine. We give them buggers good time I reckon.

Crook grinned and spoke, waving his hand.

You see? said Batman. Even the Parramattas have stomach for a fight. And them free men already. You bastards might not wear chains but by God you are shackled.

They pondered on that across a moment.

I'm for it, said Baxter.

As am I, said Gumm.

Horsehead spat on the blackened grass. Better chained than buried I say. We was lucky last time, lucky them cannibals never found us. That's the head and tail of it.

You think he'll let you stay on as a hand? said Gumm. He'll have you carted back to Campbell Town lockup, wont he?

There's worse in life than prison bars, Gummy.

All eyes shifted onto him as he kneaded the blue obelisk inked on his knuckles and rocked to and fro on his haunches. Around him a thousand thin smokes rose like stalks of wheat from the smouldering ashes. All right, he said after a length, I'll do it. Fer that blasted ticket.

Batman crushed the letter in his fist. Then let us strike out tomorrow, he said.

DAYBREAK SAW THE ASSIGNEES STUFFING THEIR skin drums with the necessaries of bush life. They were loaded, each man, with what he could carry by way of powder and shot until their lean backs bent beneath the weight and their mutterings grew. When William Gould arrived at their cookfires, rednosed and shivering, he had a half-dozen pair of leather prison slippers tied up in a sack and he walked among the men dispensing them. The slippers hung flaccid and grey as if sewn from the skin of old dugs.

Jimmy Gumm took a pair in his hand and looked them over. What's this?

It's shoes, said Gould.

Be damned if it is.

Near as you'll get at least.

It aint near. It aint shoes.

Better than bare feet.

Gumm looked over his shoulder. You hear that, Horse? Better than bare feet he says.

Tell that maggot he can shove his slippers up his ringhole.

See? Even Horsehead says you can shove yer slippers.

Gould hawked snot in his throat and spat.

Nonetheless they took those poor shoes and they crouched and unwound the puttees from their legs and tossed the grimy rags onto the fire where they blackened and smouldered. The boy wedged his foot inside one slipper and split the sole clear through the heel. A moment before he'd appeared wholly sat-isfied at his turn of luck but now he thumped the earth and ripped the slipper off his foot, tossing it to burn beside his rags. The other men fitted the little things upon their feet, clasped between thumb and forefinger in a dainty motion of the hand akin to a lady pulling on her hose, and they all glanced around and stared at Gould.

...

The sunlight burned through the window hole and Katherine passed before it aglow. Bill squinted as she set a mug of sassafras tea near his hand. He hacked some meat off a wallaby leg for her and they ate and watched smoke unfurl out the hole in the siding. Bill removed the tea and sugar rations from his drum and gave them to her, the best cuts of mutton also. The tobacco he kept. She took them quietly.

We could be gone a month or more, he said.

She raised her eyes.

When he stood he pushed back his chair and lifted the doorflap on its leather hinges. Katherine followed him outside into the morning. A chimerical mist remained caught upon the gums and it tore as he moved through it. He settled his knapsack and his almighty fowling piece across his shoulders and sucked a draught of the freezing air. There he stood a moment, studying the scrub. He walked a slow circle of the humpy between the stumps of felled trees long gone grey with age. His woman stared.

They'll approach from that way, he said. He pointed up the shallow incline where the scrub grew stouter and more gloomy than elsewhere. She looked up at the blue gums trailing peels of bark from their limbs.

Keep plenty of water inside. They'll be looking to burn you out.

She made no reply but her breath beaded pearl white.

Dont leave the hut without a gun. If they see that it's the end of you.

And he went to her and held her hand for a long while. The two of them standing in the forest ruins in silence. Then he set off into the bush alone.

. . .

They went with the leaden hearts of men who knew what a hundred miles was and saw it stretched never-ending across days into weeks before them. Eliza was ringed by her girls and they raised their hands in farewell and watched the party slog up the mud track. Crossing the hill the men were skylit and their shadow forms rose over the crest then vanished. They left behind an emptiness the bleating of sheep and the hollering of children could not fill. Eliza shielded her eyes and scanned the paddocks and the scrub stands and the sky in every direction. It was country riddled with the bruised souls of a decade's war and although she could not see them she knew they were there, walking their trails, voices intermingled in song, bearing spears meant for her and her children. She turned and herded the girls indoors.

THE PARTY CUT ALONG THE ROAD'S centre where the sunken ruts of cartwheels lay in dark parallel. Each man labouring under forty pound of packweight in a rambling single file. They walked gentle park that morning, country far removed from the tangle and suffocation of Ben Lomond's foothills. Everywhere they looked across that wooded grassland leapt boomers by the hundreds, great bounding beasts like cattle gone mad, and John Batman made a sport of potting them over great distances by firing from one knee or on the move, it mattered not which. The wounded roos made strange moans and they kicked their legs like dogs deep in dream and scores of crows descended from the sky to gather about the dead, tail feathers in the air, gobs of ruby-red meat flapping in their beaks.

Around noon the company found themselves on a stark plain. It rolled away to the hills south and east and was barren of everything save sheep. They passed through flocks of ewes fording the road and through a cloying fleece stench as that broad white river opened and closed again behind them. Bigboned meat sheep of the sort Batman ran on his own farm as feed for the government stores and the chain gangs. Their wool good for nothing but stuffing ceiling cavities. They mewled stupidly in the cold and clipped at the grass and their demon's eyes never blinked.

In the far-off a figure could be made out against the green fields holding his arm high in salute. At first they supposed him to be the shepherd but as they neared they saw the barrel-chest he was standing beside and his highnecked shirt and waistcoat and they looked around at each other in query. He was alone upon that plain with neither rifle nor pistol, alone and stationed beside the cart ruts that were the only bit of civilisation anywhere. He waved and when he spoke he had the airs of society and the men came to a halt some yards off and stared at him.

I'd thought you might have forgotten me, said the toff.

John Batman leaned on his weapon and looked the fellow up and down. He was hatless and his jacket was laid over the chest to sit on. Batman turned to his men. What's he talkin about?

Must be a drunk, said Gould. Or a madman.

I was expecting you an hour ago. But never mind. You are here now. Shall we move off? The toff mopped his forehead with a lace handkerchief which he stuffed back into his breast pocket. He knocked on the lid of the chest. You should be able to manage it between you.

John Batman grinned. He produced his pouch and took a pinch for his cheek and as he worked it around his jaw he brought his gun off his back. He held it slackly as if he meant nothing by it.

There's trouble to be had in these parts, he said.

Sheep wandered blindly in the fields. The toff studied the Dharug men and the Vandemonian and he smiled and nodded but they offered nothing to him by way of reply. They crouched in the grass and watched him through thin eyes. Now he looked across the other faces in Batman's posse and the questions forming in his mind seemed to find expression in the knitting of his brow. Sweat trickled down his cheeks as he studied the six-foot fowling pieces and the knives and pistols with which they were armed and the hides draped upon their persons like the vandals of old Rome. He cleared his throat.

I would wager that you chaps represent not the smallest of it, he said.

You have that right, said Batman.

The toff pulled out his lace handkerchief and dabbed at his upper lip. I am to meet a Mr. Wedge here. He assured me a buggy would be waiting.

Seems it aint.

Are you chaps heading somewheres?

No.

Well I should think a militia such as this surely serves some purpose?

Purpose. We're full of that, said Batman. Brimming with it.

Then I wonder if you might not escort me to John Wedge's property. I'd happily pay for your time.

John Batman stared at him. You have a name?

Dawson.

Take heed now, Mr. Dawson. Even a feckless arse like you should see that if any one of us old boys wants yer money he shall take it. Wont be nothin you can do against it. Not a damn thing.

The toff clutched the handkerchief to his chest, his eyes broad and white as they darted from man to man. With his gun Batman gestured at the travelling chest in the grass. What have you got in there then?

The toff glanced over his shoulder and all around. Looked for help someplace on that bald plain. But there was nothing, no one.

What is this? said the toff.

Batman spat to the side. It is what it is, he said.

There was something sinister in his tone, something weighty. The toff watched him. He fished a little ring of keys from his waistcoat and turned one in the brass lock set in the oakwood. He raised the lid. With his eyes still fixed on the fellow Batman slung his gun and stepped closer to the trunk. He stood and studied its contents a moment. He looked at the toff. He bent down and placed a hand inside the chest and riffled through the innards. It was lined with red velvet and hung inside the lid were deerskin straps finished in buckles cast from silver and it was perfumed with lavender and rose oil and polished with beeswax. Batman chewed his baccy as he stared into the depths of that chest. Then he stood and moved away.

My apologies, he said to the toff, but the toff would not look at him. He pressed the handkerchief to his mouth and the knotted corners caught on the wind. Batman nodded at him. I hope you aint left here too long.

No, wait, he said, but they did not. Wait. I will pay.

Batman called the men onwards. The party put along the cloven road once more with Batman at their head and they watched the toff diminish on that long plain until he was a texture on the field. In the wheel ruts the water teemed with polliwogs and the men walked the fringes of the track, their slippers sodden. They paced behind Batman and waited for him to speak but he said nothing. He stared straight ahead, beating out the miles. It was Horsehead who finally addressed the question to him, at the insistence of the rest. He fell in beside Batman, rubbed his running nose on his sleeve and coughed. All was silent except the suck of their feet sloughing in the mud.

So now, he said, why dont you tell us. Tell us what was in there.

Batman fingered the tobacco from his cheek and flicked the clod spinning out across the plain. He looked Horsehead in the eye.

Was it grog?

Batman walked on unhurried.

Some Chinese soporific then, wasnt it?

They'd covered a dozen yards or so before Batman said anything more and in the wash of light spilling through the clouds he appeared strangely serene. We must learn from life how to suffer it with dignity, he said. But I tell you, that bloke has some learning to do yet.

. . .

In the afternoon the company reached a creek edging the grasslands to the south where the forest walled off the plain and the chirruping of frogs sounded out the seconds. All of the party men placed their feet with care as they went among the stones near the water as it was known that snakes bred there in profusion. The creek itself was a dull trickle. The rovers refilled their canteens and drank as the frogs piped mindlessly in the shallows. Along the road further they passed a cete of badgers moving away as the men approached. The badgers had burrows on the plain and laboured off to these diggings. Some buried only their heads, leaving their bodies exposed. The assignees kicked at the animals but the badgers were as solid as barrels and clung to the earth with inch-long claws. The men kicked and dragged at the stumpy legs but the animals huddled up tighter into circles.

John Batman came alongside Bill to pass him a canteen. They stood together in the saplings grown high along the grassed embankment and watched the men at their foolery. It was untended country, unburned. There were wiry stems, the very beginnings of trees, sprouting in the soil. Gums for the most part, as sheep refused their bitter leaves, but blackwoods as well. Little stands of tea-trees too placed about as if by some enormous hand. All bending in the weather.

Batman screwed up his eyes in the low winter sun. I'd say the blacks have given up on this pasture.

Bill drank again from the canteen and recorked it as he began walking off along the track. They can no more give it up than you can give up yer hands and feet, he said.

. . .

The party was a few miles short of St Paul's Plains when the weather turned bitter. The cloud cover swelled darkly over an hour and when the rain hit it came like stones thrown against the earth, great fistfuls flung in anger, and it was deafening. The men huddled shivering under their blankets, as wet as ship's rats, and looked out upon a world turned foul. Only Black Bill stayed on his feet with the sleet collecting on the brim of his hat while beyond him at the horizon the cloud banks scuffed Ben Lomond frigid white. On dark the rain eased to a mist and Batman had them pitch an oiled canvas lean-to he'd packed from knowledge of the weather. The makings of a fire were hard to come by so Crook used his knife to strip the bark off some branches and carve raised scales along one end. He took a portion of the dried punk carried as tinder—a habit learned from the local tribes—and before long had a fire sizzling. The men twisted water from their blankets in pairs and then put their clothes inside the blankets and wrung the water out of them too. It was a wretched business and their teeth rattled in their jaws as they piled under the canvas as near to the fire as practicable while they watched the billycan come to the boil.

Sixteen hundred and ninety-two, said Gumm.

Baxter passed him a pannikin. William the Third.

Fourteen hundred and seventy.

Henry the Sixth's second reign, said Baxter. You'll have to do better than that.

Thirteen hundred and fifty-one.

Edward the Third.

Uncanny.

How far back can you go? said the boy.

Harold Harefoot reliably. Although I have some knowledge before that, tis a mite untrustworthy.

Nine hundred and sixty, said Horsehead.

Well now. That's a better test. Edgar the Peaceable I believe it was.

What else you know? said the boy.

Baxter was sitting on his knapsack and he leaned forward

between his gangling legs. I knew a Glaswegian what marked the place where my cow's buried, he said.

The boy frowned at him. The assignees looked at each other, blankfaced, unable to locate Baxter's meaning.

Jimmy Gumm was first to make a stab at it. He squinted at Baxter with his bad eye. You, he said, who was to be put from the gibbet for effectin a robbery under arms? You owned a cow?

Mike Howe I said. Mike Howe. Murderous governor of the woods. I aint never owned no cow nor bloody will I.

Spit them Welsh rocks out of your mouth we might understand a bloody word.

I said twas an old Scotchman who was showed the resting place of Mike Howe or so he told me.

John Batman tapped his pipe out on his boot. His head or his body?

Well now. I suppose it must have been his body.

You cant call it a grave then.

I never called it a grave.

What happened to his head? said the boy.

The Governor had it mounted, lad, said Batman.

The party men drew their wet blankets around their shoulders and listened to the anguished breeze swirl. God rest him, said Baxter.

A mournful silence drew over that campsite as they one and all considered the fate that had befallen Howe. They looked into their pannikins and rubbed their whiskers or crossed themselves.

THEY BARELY SLEPT AND WHEN MORNING came it broke so dim and grey that the sun was full up before they woke. They set out along the road and ate and drank as they walked, strips of cold fried mutton and a canteen of tea passing between them.

At St. Paul's Plains they found a scene that sank their spirits further. Pools of standing water as vast and metallic as lakes covered the grassland. Adrift on the ponds like sodden pillows were small lambs and Jimmy Gumm waded in and caught one up but found the meat bloated beyond use. He threw the pitiful carcass back into the water where it sank in a stream of bubbles.

A corridor of drooping oak followed the South Esk River across the width of the plains and the company reached those few trees alongside the riverbanks and there they were brought to a stop. The river had swollen into a broad barricade and each man looked at the others and they all looked at John Batman for his say-so. He surveyed that sliding wall east to west but there was no way across.

Well I'll be meanly buggered, he said.

They walked downstream a few hundred yards for want of anything better to do and John Batman bade them to watch for a narrowing where they might cross. Little scrub wrens hopped along the ground after insects but took wing as the men neared. They had covered not more than a quarter-mile when Bill suddenly yanked off his knapsack and tossed it across the flow. As one the men stopped walking and watched him. He unlaced his boots and lobbed them onto the far bank and then he dived headlong into the rapids and came up bearing his hat in one hand as he powered for the bank. He found a handhold in the drowned brush of the riverbank and dragged himself ashore. Batman chuckled at first and looked around at the other men and soon he was laughing fullchested at the display Bill had made.

You want to learn a thing or two boys, he said, just watch how old Billy does it. He unwound a hemp rope and cast it over to Bill and Bill tied it off. One after another the men shimmied across, trailing their legs in the flow. On the far bank Bill caught their wrists and raised them up, each likewise until only Horsehead stood on the north bank. He had a sickly air about him and would not approach the water.

Take good grip of that, called Batman. Or you'll be lost.

Horsehead's look of distress was comic. That he was a man divided against himself was plain to see. He tried to approach the river by inching forward holding his bundled effects yet he could move no closer. He stared at the slack line drawn above the torrent and shook his head.

A steady drizzle fell upon Batman's hat and the kangaroo fur of his bag. He gazed up at the sky as if asking what new hardship would befall him next. Then he seized his weapon and started off along the southern plain and his men followed him.

Here, said Horsehead. Where youse goin?

No one answered.

Here now.

The men kept walking. Horsehead stepped a little closer to the river and when he spoke the rushing of the floodwater filled the hollows between his words. I cant swim, he called. Hold on. Darnt leave me.

Horsehead picked up a rock and threw it and it clattered in the brush beside Bill. On the far bank the Vandemonian swung about. Water ran off the brim of his hat as he stared across the deluge.

You'll help a man in need wont you, Bill?

Bill was silent.

You done me a good turn back on that mountain. You saved me from them cannibals. Do us one more wont you?

I ought to have left you up there.

No sense in havin that on yer conscience. You have an honest heart. Such things weigh heavy on a chap.

I aint that honest.

No, course you aint.

Bill unshouldered his piece and dropped it in the undergrowth. Make that rope fast around your waist, he said. I can haul you across.

Haul you across he says.

Then rot there.

No no no.

Bill stared at him.

All right, I'll do it. Just dont go drownin me.

Horsehead untied the rope from the branch upon which it was strung. He fastened it around his waist and made at the front a little figure-eight bend, his fingers working as slow and precise as spider legs in the cold. He waited there, arms upheld as if to ask what came next, until Bill took up the rope and yanked on it.

Horsehead stumbled forward. Bill repeated the measure and the old lag was dragged headlong into the flood. He flailed on the end of his tether, mouth agape at the sky and churning up the brown water with his panic. Bill reeled him in, hand over hand, and the river crashed over him and he was carried some way downstream. Whenever his head broke the surface a stifled cry sounded around the riverbanks like the bleatings of a newborn foal. As he drew within reach Bill released the rope and caught him up by the collar and heaved him ashore.

Horsehead coughed and gagged. He looked up. I oughta cut yer bleedin neck, you animal fucker.

But Bill was coiling the rope between his thumb and his

elbow and he neither turned nor did he hurry as he hung the rope over his arm. He found his piece in the brush and cut out for the rainsoaked plain. Horsehead watched Bill pull away as the river growled behind him and the rain fell ever more solidly and soon he stood up and followed.

. . .

A sky the colour of chiselled stone weighed down and rain pelted down on them. It was country marked out by the derelict huts of assigned shepherds long driven off by the clans. They passed one large homestead built on the labour of the same assignees, a structure incongruous with the landscape, formed out of bluestone and discordant angles. A three-legged dog hobbled out to meet them in the paddocks and Black Bill whistled to it but the beast flattened its ears and bared its teeth and the bald pink scar at its shoulder quivered. They studied that house and the ink stain of smoke above it for a time before moving on, following the river where it cut across the plain. The same river that would take them clean through to Swanport. Everywhere on the plain signs of the clans were present. Burned into the face of the country as surely as shapes were branded onto animal stock.

You've lost them.

Bill pushed back his hat. He looked around at Horsehead. You are a piece of work, he said.

Havent you?

No I have not.

I'm claimin it as fact.

Their tracks run up this way. We'll find them.

Christ but it's cold.

Just keep moving.

The sun had a few hours left to run and the rain had eased off. For a good long while Horsehead said nothing at all but he shivered and hacked like a consumptive and they walked for some miles more through the afternoon shadows before he spoke again.

What a pitiful place to be buried at.

Black Bill spat on the grass.

Here in the wilds. Buried and unmourned.

Aye. Who would mourn a thief?

Me boys. They would mourn their father if they was given to know the place of his grave. But they will never know it.

They continued along the river. In some parts it spilled free of its banks and spread dull brown tendrils out across the plain and they waded through these offshoots up to their thighs with the current eddying around them. Swimming in one of these spills was a sleek black snake the length and breadth of a leather belt and Bill caught hold of Horsehead to stop him as it wound past, a spread of ripples clearing in its wake.

You have boys? said Bill.

Wet clothes sucked at their skin as they walked in the tracks of the roving party.

Four. The eldest bein nineteen years.

Some minutes of quiet passed between them. Then Horsehead raised his eyes. Yerself?

I've a boy comin along.

But you know it's a boy?

I know it is.

How's that then?

How's what?

How do you know it's a boy?

Bill eyed him through the drizzle. I was told so.

They climbed a low grassed hill and stood on top leaning into the wind. In the near distance a huge signal fire burned and men could be seen moving across the blaze in peaceful silhouette. Bill and Horsehead stood beside each other, their shadows lengthening in the twilight as they silently assessed the final country left for them to cover. Upon dusk they walked into Batman's camp. The rovers were sat at rest on a thinly scrubbed hill near the river and they watched the latecomers drop their drums and warm themselves at the blaze. They stood backed to that fire dunking damper into fresh tea and eating it still dripping. John Batman had for himself a jar of pickled onions which he popped one after another into his mouth and crunched along with his damper while the last of the daylight died along the horizon. He looked at Horsehead as he popped another onion.

Decent debt you have buildin up with Bill there.

Horsehead licked crumbs from his whiskers. He's a good sort. For a darkie.

He's worth ten ayou. Batman rolled the onion in his cheek.

They all watched Horsehead. His clothes steamed with the fire's heat.

It's the last time I aid his sorry deeds, said Bill.

You hear that? Even the black's turned on you.

Horsehead gazed around the faces shining in the fire glow. They'll bury us all out here anyways, said Horsehead. The lot of us.

Your chance might come sooner than you reckon, said Batman and he crunched another onion.

THE RIVER WENT EVER ONWARDS AND the company with it. In all directions the grasslands spread green and glistening and the prints of wallabies and native badgers were tracked plainly in the wet. Every dozen yards or so along the flanks of the river they scared up teams of emus that bolted away on their long horse's legs. Crook found duck nests hidden in the thickets and the men drank down the eggs as they walked the sparsely wooded country. The rain was gone away to the west and although no sun shone the air was warmer for the change. They walked strung out in a line beside the river, each with his head down watching the ground for snakes.

But some time before noon they found themselves no longer among living gum trees but instead passing stands of mighty deadwoods bearing the deep wounds of ringbarking. Overhead the churning charcoal sky was visible where the foliage ought to have spread and in the birdless silence those bones creaked and scraped. At length they happened upon a farmhouse, a rude construction of split logs roofed with bark weighed down by spars. There were wooden buckets of water stood every place around the house, likely as proof against the tossing of fire-sticks by the blacks, for this was well known as hostile country. John Batman stood off eyeing the hut and looking sour.

There's a fire at least, said Gould, pointing at the chimney and the white smoke spewing from it.

They crossed a hundred yards of limp potato plants chipped in among the dead gums and when they came close enough Batman called out to the shack. Three lean dogs staked by the door set to whining. A flap of bark swung outwards and a fellow appeared on the door stone. He was garbed in brown-grey pelts and he wore on his feet hide moccasins like oversized socks. The piece hanging on rope over his shoulder had had its stock remade in some rawcut native timber. He studied the strangers, keeping the muzzle levelled upon them.

You come to kill me? he said.

We dont mean to kill no bastard.

Bushrangers most probably. Aint youse?

Well we aint, said Batman.

No concern of mine what you are. The fellow looked from man to man then back to Batman. None at all, he said. He gripped his rifle, taking stock of their weaponry and gazing long at the black men.

Might we make use of yer fire?

What's yer business here?

John Batman spat to the side. We're out for some blackbirding, he said.

On the straight?

Batman just looked at him.

I tell you now, there's nothing here worth the taking. If you mean to rob me.

Batman slung his shotgun, signalled his party men to do likewise. We've been a good while on these plains, he said. His dry throat bore more of a husk than ever. We'd appreciate the use of your fire. To warm up.

Them blacks tame?

Not as much as you would hope.

Wouldnt have a tot of rum about your person I spose?

No rum but tobacco and sugar and tea, said Batman.

The fellow cursed at the dogs to be quiet. He waited in his doorway as the party approached. Batman put out his hand.

John Batman, he said over the dogs.

Henry Ridewood, said the man.

They shook.

Ridewood looked again at the Vandemonian and he dipped his forehead towards the black men, a small and secret gesture. Tryin to better themselves are they? he said to Batman in a low voice.

Dont be fooled by a few clothes.

Well leavem out here. I wont have blacks inside me hut.

The assignees downed their knapsacks and followed him

inside and the Dharugs and Black Bill watched them depart. A lively sun had appeared so they shifted into its warmth to wait. The hunting dogs yawled and raised their hackles much as did every other white man's dog in that occupied country when they sighted a black man. The threesome held their weapons to their chests and waited.

Henry Ridewood was a man of few means. Wallaby skins staked and dried lay heaped in the corners of the shack and the party men, upon finding nowhere to sit, planted themselves atop those piles. The billy was offered around and the men drank from the lip and gave muted thanks. A homely fire burned that lit the room. It was close inside the hut and the stench of animal pelts hid every other smell. The smoke drew mostly up the chimney but a decent amount drifted free and turned the air in the shack soupy and setting Horsehead off on a round of coughing. He hawked into his palm and smeared the mess on his trousers.

We heard word of blacks being hereabouts, said Batman.

Ridewood nodded. His expression hardened. You heard right.

You seen them?

Seen em. Talked with em. Traded with em. Regular as shipmates we are, me and them blackfolks. He pointed out the doorway to the country of dead trees curving away into a plain a quarter-mile south where there seemed no sign of anything man or animal. They live down thataways.

How many?

A few. Bigguns and littluns. Naked as French whores the lot of them. But they's friendly enough.

So you never had no trouble?

None worth the word. They call after tea and grub and what have you so I give what I can spare. For use of the land unmolested, you see. They wont tolerate me on their hunting lands but here in the scrub. Well. Seems they oblige, dont it?

At that point Ridewood reached inside his clothes and fished out a tobacco pouch and he handed it around to the men who opened the drawstring and peered inside but it proved to be empty. They passed it around to Batman.

What is it?

Crow skin.

John Batman pulled the leather through his fingertips. It was supple. Pored like chicken.

Thigh flesh suits best if you mean to tan it I'm told. Ridewood stirred the billy then replaced it in the ashes of the meagre fire. But that there is the bawbag of some poor black fool.

Batman looked anew at the pouch. It maintained the shape of genitals. He wrong you? This chap?

Ridewood took the pouch from him then stuffed it back inside his tunic. Not me, said Ridewood. There was this emancipist lived on the river some years back. A decent old cuss. It was him what made it.

Name of Gunshannon?

160

That's him.

I heard told he was dead.

He is. Saw that with me own two eyes. He had it comin his way if any chap ever did. He was one for shootin the blacks he was. Had himself a pack of rooing dogs trained for the purpose and kept lively by the constant application of the lash. Him and his dogs scoured those hills aways south, the Sugarloaf, the Tiers, and shot every sorry fool they saw. Took his trophies from em. Those of us what knew the blacks warned him off out of it. They'll hold a grudge in their miserable hearts long past sense or reason we told him. But away he went after roo and whatever savages were daft enough to cross him. Sure as eggs they got him one day when he was comin in. Put a twelve-foot spear straight through him. They poison em, you know. Stand the tips in rotten offal. It was one such that he caught in the gut.

The men on the piles of skins looked around at each other and shifted uneasily on their seats.

Ridewood continued: He crawled to his hut did this eman-cipist and he proceeded to die across a few days. A proper bloody horror it was. Near the end he lost his mind. He'd scream out how the blacks was circlin his bed and kick off his bedclothes. We tended to him but nothin earthly could be done for his health. A proper horror I tell you. No way for a man to die. Even a man like Gunshannon.

You find them animals what did it? said the boy.

I left well enough alone, son.

You'd kill a dog what bit you, wouldnt you?

That false courage'll vanish when faced with them spears.

A leg of wallaby meat was hanging to smoke in the fireplace and Ridewood gestured at it now. You lads want some grub?

They nodded. He unhooked the claw and using a string-handled fisherman's knife lay a few slices of the shiny crimson meat onto a board and pushed it across the table. The assignees fell on it like house rats.

You aim to thin their numbers yerself then? He directed this at John Batman.

Batman's hat was upturned in his hand and he looked inside the dark well of the crown and measured his answer. We'll see.

Ridewood seemed to expect him to say something more.

Batman cleared his throat and obliged him. We hear one name spoken on here and there. Manalargena.

Ridewood sat back in his chair. He ran his eyes across the six crowded into his hut. Took account of them. He nodded his head. I see. You blokes are come after the witch.

Batman folded his arms and stared.

Then youse are better men than I.

I've met lepers that was a better sort than some of this lot, said Batman.

That man has a meanness even God wont forgive.

Does he now?

Believe it.

Batman looked around at his men and they at him. We aint no trifles ourselves, he said.

He will come upon you like the flame of fire. I tell you now. Wont no sidearms will save ye.

You think us faint hearts, said Gumm. Choose yer words, Ridewood. There's some short tempers in here.

I'm not questionin yer mettle.

Then think hard on what you say next.

The billy rattled in the coals of the fireplace and Ridewood leaned down slowly and with his bare hand he lifted the can and sat it on the hearthstone. When he turned to look at them his face was lit in the ember glow. He licked his lips. I dont doubt what you are. None ayou. But if you provoke the snake, you must prepare to get bit. Know this. He will teach you the truest lesson you ever learned.

They took a last round of stringent bush tea in silence then John Batman rose and donned his hat and stepped into the warming afternoon with his men behind him. They waited as Batman surveyed the country ahead and Ridewood followed them down and offered some counsel about the most advantageous way to proceed. Out of boredom Black Bill was working his blade through his fingers, spun like a palmist's coin across his knuckles, around his thumb. Ridewood watched as he caught the blade.

carner mema lettenner? Ridewood said to him. Each sound emerged poorly formed.

The Vandemonian didn't look up but fed the knife into its hide sheath and laid it across his knee. Panninher, he said.

You speak somethin of his cant? said Jimmy Gumm.

Somethin.

You speak Welsh any? We need someone to tell our Taffy he stinks like a flyblown arse.

But the old fellow proffered nothing by way of that matter; his gaze was fixed upon the Vandemonian and the broad dagger on his knee. He addressed Black Bill once more. nina Tummer-ti narapa?

Bill looked him full in the eye. narapa.

I knew as much. Knew it by the look of you. The blackfolk have many names for you as well but there's few they will speak.

They speak them clear enough when it suits. Bill clutched the sheathed knife in his fist.

The company walked once more into the woodlands. Ridewood whistled his dogs off and collared them with loops of rawhide and he stood staring after the party for a long while.

. . .

They tracked that whole afternoon across a series of sandy plains where nothing grew save tussocks of speargrass. The ground underfoot was softened by rain and adhered to their slippered feet. Puddle water mirrored the ragged shreds of cloud and the boy shattered the images one then another and another until he was mud to the knees. But the men ignored his madness, instead looking east where those same clouds were displacing around the peaks of the rainforested hills they'd be climbing by tomorrow. The Dharugs scouted the soundest terrain and led the company along.

In following the Parramatta men the party was spread thin over a mile or so and after a while Black Bill turned to tally the bobbing heads. He made it seven. Another count brought the same result. So he put his hand to his eyes and searched the stretch funnelling away down the valley. Standing rigid among a stand of tussocks was William Gould. He did not reply when Bill cooeed to him and he remained erect, outlined against the dark hills like a stone sentinel, his coat flapping and his hair flattened in the wind. Black Bill unslung his weapon and removed the oilcloth from the firing mechanism.

Hold up, he called to the front markers and the party men came to a stop and faced him.

The Vandemonian trudged the hundred yards back to Gould, scanning the few shrubs marking that flat land and holding his gun at his waist. A pair of plovers cackled and swooped with their golden wattles ashine in the sun. When he drew up he saw that Gould was staring down at the ground. Bill lowered his gun. A great length of black snake was coiled and contorting in the grass between Gould's legs, one of the man's feet pinning the snake to the ground.

Kill it kill it kill it, he said. Sweat tracked down Gould's cheeks.

Bill crouched down. Gould's leg was quivering with the effort as he brought all his weight to bear on the trunk and the head snapped about as it searched for purchase on Gould's calf.

The Vandemonian stood up and rubbed his bare chin. You're in a bind there, he said.

Jesus, Mary and—

Just keep the pressure on it. Hold it there.

Me leg is givin out.

I said hold it.

I'm holdin, I'm holdin.

The snake whipped around.

Oh Jesus, oh dear lord.

He cant get at you. Just keep pushing.

John Batman had jogged up by now bearing his weapon but he would come no closer than a few yards.

What'll I do? Gould said to him.

Batman shook his head. You're a goner, mate.

Oh. Oh lord.

I had a dog die of snake bite. Horrible it was.

Gould's leg juddered. Shoot the blighter, wont you? he said.

Little tike clean bit his tongue off in the convulsions.

Help me, you bastards, I cant hold him.

He's eight foot if he's an inch, said Batman.

Biggest I ever saw, said Bill.

Look at that head, would you? All right. Watch yerself there.

Batman levelled the bores of his gun upon the coiled mass

and thumbed back both hammers until they settled on their locks and he was taking some sort of caution about blasting off Gould's legs when Black Bill placed a wide brown hand on the barrels. He pushed the gun aside.

We dont kill them, he said.

We? I most certainly do, my dusky friend.

But Bill would enter into no more discourse. He crouched near the snake and approached it out of eyesight. He caught the swaying head behind the jaws and then he shoved Gould off with his other hand. The whole sleek black eight feet wound up his arm and he stood with the throttled snake in his fist utterly forestalled. Two bared fangs oozed like dripping stalactites. The snake twisted and wrenched about but it was useless against Bill's locked fingers. He brought the head around to face Batman who shied off and raised his arm up.

Dont bring it near me, fer Christsake.

Then Bill flung the length of it up and away from himself and it turned a lazy circle, crashing into the speargrass some yards off, where it could be seen breaking for the tussocks nearby. William Gould bowed his head towards Bill in thanks. He came close and put out his hand. It hung between them a few moments before Bill shook it in his own.

I thought meself a dead man.

Check yer legs. To be sure.

Gould rolled up his tattered pants and felt all over his calves.

Who's we? said Batman.

Bill turned and walked off.

Yer black brothers? Batman called. You aint no part athat no more. Just you remember.

But Bill didn't look back.

...

At the mouth of a wooded gorge where blueberry ash shaded an underwood of infant man fern John Batman raised his hat and with it bade them all to halt. In unison the company set down their knapsacks. Each man in turn filled his pannikin from the eddying rockpools then lay about at ease on the banks plucking leeches from their ankles and flicking them into the river. Baxter moved among the men squeezing a wetted head of tobacco over their bite wounds, the dark juice a poison against poison. The river crept along a bed of stone and from it rose a fine brume which dampened their beards and hung dusty in the sun. They ate mutton chops, quiet but for the licking of fingers, and they watched up the slopes of the gorge for blacks until the night took them whole.

IT WAS BILL WHO LED THE party through the hills. The only map he possessed was the roll of the land, the bend of the river and the arc of the sun. This was familiar country to him. He led them that morning along St Paul's River but as it branched away he put into the forest and the party followed. Stands of dollybush and cutting grass and dogwood thrived on the hillsides and grew impenetrable so that the party was made to weave about. As they ascended the shallow incline the Vandemonian soon drew far ahead and the scrub gave around him and his bootsteps sounded out a cadence on the stones. He cooeed the party from the hilltop and when they looked up to call in return he was as featureless as shadow before the pure blue sky.

Come noon the company rested together in a valley while John Batman sought counsel from a battered brass compass. He turned it around, turned himself around, but allowed that he was none the wiser for it. Black Bill nominated a spiny rise of hills as his bearing guide and said it would take them

169

mainly south. When they moved on again the boy stuck close by Bill's side and put to him questions concerning the taking of direction from sun or moon. Bill answered patiently and expounded upon the skill of memorising a landscape which a man needed to master if he was to survive in the back countries. On sighting a grove of native cherry he plucked a handful of the currants. They ate and walked and the boy asked his questions, questions such that Bill had been asked time and again. Did he ever eat babies like other blacks? If he took to his skin with soap would the black come off? The boy waited for Bill to answer.

The party pushed on, following the Vandemonian ever deeper into the hills. A wind had tossed the canopy all day and it stiffened slowly over the afternoon and cooled, the first crisp balls of rain hitting their hats like ripe gumnuts loosed in the winds. John Batman called for the finding of shelter and the building of fires and the party men spread outwards for whatever harbour might be found in those scrubwoods. The rain was firing down when Crook showed John Batman the burnt swamp gum, pointing and chattering in the language of his countrymen. Batman ducked inside the cavern. Scorched and stinking of rot, a rubble of bones on the earth, it was indeed a fair sort of place to make an encampment so he called the men inside. Rain battered the tree's hull as the men spread out their blankets and removed their skin shoes and shook the water from their jerkins. A ring of rocks was set in the centre where Crook made them a fire. The smoke ran away obligingly up the open trunk and they draped their clothes to dry beside the flames. They were nicely settled when the boy noticed Black Bill stood in the rain a good few yards off.

The boy waved to him. Come on then.

Bill didn't move.

Batman put his head outside into the rain. What's your game? he called.

Bill was standing beside another swamp gum of much the same immense proportions, save being unburned. Water poured off his hat brim as he passed a hand down the trunk and the carvings running crossways into the tree's meat caught the points of his fingers. Bisected circles and halfmoons and spirals. The signs of life. No other tree was burned. Just one amid the many. He surveyed the great charred stump rooted into the soil and the cragged ruined branches and the smoke rising from the hollow and he knew it for what it was. He knew it for a cremation site.

So he trudged away between the gums collecting scraps of bark and branches and he heaped them leewards of a rock mantle as the rain streamed off his limbs. The men watched him work, their mutton upraised on sticks above the cook fire. Bill fashioned a rude breakwind against the ledge with leafy branches of eucalypt then he wedged himself out of the weather. Lightning lit the cloud cover in a series of short argent bursts. The rain had hardened and the death drum of thunder rolled on. The Vandemonian felt its reverberations in the solid earth beneath him.

Pigeon stepped outside into the weather and walked through the rain, bending his head into the breakwind. He grinned at Bill and Black Bill grinned back.

Come eat, old man, he said.

Not in there.

You want grub?

Bill shrugged.

Pigeon crossed through the gale and when he re-emerged he had in one hand the billycan and in the other a portion of damper and he set them before the Vandemonian.

Batman say you bloody mad.

No more than he I should think.

He turned to study the burnt cavern and the fire glow on those bearded faces. He stuffed a crust of damper in his mouth and chewed and Pigeon sat under the shelter with him as the blind storm thrashed wildly into the hillside.

THEY PUSHED ON ALL MORNING DOWN a gorge and coming up the far side, a densely wooded incline, they chanced upon a rock overhang stained with the soot of countless cook fires. Nearby was a midden comprised of possum and wallaby bones and the carapace of crayfish, likely taken from the creek below, as well as hunks of broken glass, a section of shirt, a rotting blanket. The camp had not seen use in months. Batman kicked through the leavings and picked up the blanket on the tip of his knife to examine its construction. Then Crook whistled and raised his hands from the edge of the stone ground where the needlebush opened up and he waved his arms and pointed and clicked his tongue. There was a markener running up to and away from the overhang. It was a wide track, plain as cobble, following the natural movement of the land as it swelled and shrank into swale. The party men looked to John Batman and he in turn looked to Black Bill. The Vandemonian gazed about at the hills and above at the vacant sun and he studied the markener a while then began along its course. The rovers duly followed.

He led them under the waterlogged scrub which discharged a stream upon their heads as they pushed on and soon they were drenched once more to the skin. They walked out the sunless morning at a slackened pace and stopped often to sip cold tea, shivering in the shadows. The weapons hanging longwise on their backs caught on every protrusion and this more than any other nuisance riled the men to fury as they wrenched the stocks of their pieces around and yanked on their leathers. It was miserable going. They hacked up the damp within their chests and bent over and spat long strings of phlegm. Even the seasoned men of the Parramatta ceased their singing.

. . .

Black Bill found the first of the marked trees standing alone in a gully. The bark had been stripped back and the bare flesh exposed and he remained a short distance away gazing up at the mark hacked into the eucalypt as he considered its meanings. What he saw prompted him to bring his rifle off his shoulder. The party men were filed out along the trail behind him and they watched him unsling his weapon and they dropped down and snatched their pieces around likewise. He whistled John Batman over and they stood shoulder to shoulder studying that sigil and looking up and down the gully but they could make no sense of it. It was an arrow, well shaped and freshly made.

Could be splitters.

Bill pushed his hat back. There wont be clans here if bushmen are walking their roads.

Batman scuffed at the dirt with his boot heel. You think we might be in the wrong country?

If Bill held an opinion on that point he kept it to himself. He felt along the way marker with his fingers tracing over its three lines. Then he walked off down the trail. A dozen yards up they found another arrow notched into a silver wattle denoting the same direction. As the morning aged they trod the markener under them and passed at intervals the newly carved arrows where colonists had overlaid their own guide posts upon that ancestral pathway, a light serration tracing across the hills. The small stone cairns the blacks left as markers had been kicked and scattered and there was everywhere the signs of settler life. Hessian flour sacks and shards of pottery and shoes worn clean through littered the pathway or hung lodged in branches. On a hill crest they rested for a spell beneath a blue gum cloven lengthways by lightning strike, considered a lucky omen by Baxter, and they shared a pipe and watched their back trail like wanted men. What they'd supposed as a clanhold they now saw as contested country, a boundary land where one kind melded with another. They smoked and listened for footsteps.

. . .

As evening fell around them they put down a camp in a ring of mallee grown back off the path some distance. The ground was traced with the toeprints of wallabies and the balled hairy scat of devils, and the Parramatta men used the last sun to fashion spears for a hunt. From the choicest of the mallee they whittled the tips by means of Pigeon's folding knife, gripping the haft with their feet as they worked. The point was then tempered in the fire and when each had a number finished they rose and gathered them up.

You come too, old man, said Pigeon, but Black Bill looked up from the bake hole he was digging and shook his head. So the Dharugs set off into the scrub without him and the blackened points of their spears wavering above the wattle understorey was all to be seen of them.

They weren't long in pursuit. As the sunlight unwove and the forest shadows swelled the air began to fill with insects. The men slapped at their forearms and necks and someone loaded gum leaves onto the fire which smoked rankly and repelled the mosquitoes somewhat. The incessant buzz put the assignees on edge so that when the Dharugs suddenly reappeared out of the scrub one or two reached for their pieces until they saw it was Pigeon standing in the firelight and they eased their weapons down. He dragged a fresh killed kangaroo carcass up to the fireside. The men stared at him.

Found it in a tree. Them black buggers I reckon.

John Batman stood up. Where?

Not far. Plenty dog tracks down there.

Christ. Well, it's dark now. Let's have us a look in the morning.

Crook had a small wallaby that he tossed whole onto the flames. The sparks he raised swirled and turned and he clenched his eyes. He rolled the carcass to singe away the hair from every part then he scored the leg meat and emptied out the guts, smearing the intestines and stomach over the body to slow the cooking, and dumped it back onto the fire. A moon as white and full as a cross section of bone rose in the night sky. They ate the wallaby with their hands and broke the marrow from its ribs between two flat rocks. When they had finished eating they hurled the skin and offal and bones up the scrub for the devils to eat.

It was some time later when Bill awoke in the dark. He rolled out of his blanket. Pigeon and Crook were already on their feet and outlined against the bush, as faded as charcoal figurings on a cave wall, their pieces shouldered and cocked. Bill felt the ground for his own gun and stood with it, listening at the black vacancy beyond the faint cast of the fire. There was a feeble noise pulsing in the distance.

Sounds like cows, said the boy as he threw off his covers. They roused the rest. In the awful stillness the men bent their ears to the bush and strained to make out the noise. John Batman began packing fresh shot down each of his two muzzles and around him the rising and falling hiss of iron rods along barrels played out.

I cant hear nothin, said Batman. Stop it a minute.

They paused at their work.

I reckon it's possums is all.

No, not them, said Pigeon. You hear?

They raised their heads.

That's dogs, said Bill.

He's right.

If there is dogs there is blacks.

Comin closer.

Be ready for em now, said Batman.

Look dere, look dere, said Crook and the rovers swung about in surprise at those recognisable words to see him staring into the sky, and when he pointed the party men as one saw the source of his alarm. The bold disc of moon in that barren sky was shrinking. What dim light there was dissolved as the shadow spread.

What in God's name? said Batman.

The eclipsed moon's faint halo glowed but gave no light. All was as lost as if it had never been. Then the howling grew, rising and resounding in that faultless dark, and the party men raised their weapons blindly for the charge they knew was imminent. They lined up together in the throw of light from the coals that died at their feet. Beyond it was a void, so that when the first dogs burst forth they appeared as if from nothing, conjured into existence and bounding, teeth bared, for their throats. Some of the men toppled back and cried out, with ravening dogs at their arms and faces and still more beasts emerged from the darkness to catch at their rags or their limbs. Others were lost to the panic that followed and broke for the scrub with dogs tearing at them but John Batman went at the hounds with the metal butt plate of his shotgun. In the firelight the blood spewing from broken skulls ran thickly black and he trod through it and whaled into those crazed animals or tore them off his men by their scruffs.

The baying of dogs came so loud it resounded in Bill's skull as he felt about in the dark. When the first shot was fired his vision clouded and the sulfur burned in his nose. He unhooked his powder horn and dosed up the nozzle as the men called direction to one another and John Batman's burred voice cursed them on until another blazing report showed the forest briefly in daylight. A dog whimpered nearby. Black Bill crouched in shelter, waiting on the first flight of spears, but as Batman walked over to the whining dog and put one more barrel into its head the spears did not come. Bill fired at the mallee thereabouts and felled a further dog and bent to repack.

You see any? called Batman.

I see dogs.

I aint speared yet. Why aint I speared?

Off in the jetblack night they heard the screams of one man assailed by the pack. Bill went blindly forth, feeling his way with outstretched hands and making towards the shrieking. He stumbled then righted himself and felt around the wattles and through the musk bush, drawing close enough for the cries to hurt his ears but still he saw nothing. The dank smell of the frenzied dogs was everywhere in that wood as Bill hit at the underbrush and swung again, finally connecting with flesh.

Help, help, God help me.

Bill assailed the animals with wild swings, driving his booted feet in until at length the dogs relinquished and he was able to haul the fellow upright and he saw now that it was Horsehead. But the dogs came again and Bill fired his weapon square into the jaws of one that leapt at him. The pan's flash showed the eye shine of a dozen more dogs around him. He grabbed Horsehead and led him at a flat run through the trees to where the company men had regathered in the coal's halflight. They were bloodied and wrathful and armed with whatever had come to hand, stew pots, stones, sticks. Dogs stalked in the scrub at the fire's limits and a good many more lay upon the ground dead or near to. As the moon shed its shadows and the scrub was recast in pallid blues Batman cooeed into the night and it was returned by Gumm. Soon he and Baxter blundered forth from the darkness.

Me hand, said Horsehead.

He had cupped one hand under an armpit, his forearms a mess of blood, and he walked among the men seeking some kind of assistance. He came before Batman, who grabbed his hand and yanked it into the light. Horsehead cried out and cursed him. The forefinger of the left hand was gone to the knuckle. Batman turned the wound to examine it by the fire, he saw the protrusion of bone splinter and the torn skin, and he let the damaged hand fall.

I cant do nothin for it.

Christ. Me whole arm is burning.

What's that make it now? said Batman.

Eh?

Three times.

Three? Horsehead wiped his sweat.

That old Bill has delivered you from misery.

Aye. Would be that.

So there wont be no bastard to save you when he comes for payment will there? Batman walked off into the dark.

Pigeon was there and Horsehead held out his hand to him as well. What do you make of it? he said.

The Parramatta man shook his head.

Do somethin for it, wont you? Aint there a native medicine here somewhere?

How would I know? I bloody Parramatta born and raise.

What use are you then?

Shut up, you bastard, you be right.

For a while the men studied the forest. Stood with loaded arms and listened. But if there were clansfolk somewhere out in the darkness they made no sound.

Praps they was rabid. Jimmy Gumm fixed them with his good eye. I've heard an eclipse will do it to a dog.

No. They were sent, said Bill.

Rags of flame tore in the silence. In the distance the dog pack contested bones and skin, their low moans the only sound other than the fire. The men took seat around the fire and built it up from the woodheap, built up the light for what little it was, but there wasn't one among them inclined to sleep.

. . .

Come dawn they took breakfast crouched among the dog carcasses. Having little rest, the men were dark about the eyes and the boy nodded off even as he held his tea mug. It tipped forward in his grip as his head lolled and tea spilled upon the bloodfouled earth at his feet. John Batman examined the dead dogs. He found painted on the fur of some the ochre markings of the clans and he called for Bill, who came and bent over the dogs in a similar fashion. He saw in those markings the representations of kangaroo and of wallaby. In some others he saw reference to the great fables shared among the clansfolk, the stories of hunters and the creatures they slew, the designs intended to invoke the spirit of the pursuit the dogs would embark upon. He looked up at Batman.

They belong to the Plindermairhemener, he said.

What's this headman doin? Is he runnin from us? Or huntin us?

Bill fingered through the ground litter for a green gum leaf which he sucked as he spoke. You can be sure he has it reckoned out. He was born for this weather.

The Dharugs were sent out after sign of the clans. The assigned men and Bill and Batman spent the interval making ready their pieces by oiling down the iron, filing back the rust spots and cleaning the frizzens. Within the hour the Dharugs returned but they had no news. They stood about, shifting from leg to leg as Batman questioned them.

I see plenty dog track, said Pigeon.

What of the clansfolk?

They cunnin buggers. Walk them dogs through camp. All around. Now plenty dog tracks no bloody blackfella tracks.

What, none?

Maybe they rode on them dogs. Like bloody horses. Pigeon grinned. Beside him Crook held a pair of invisible reins and goaded his horse on at a trot.

Sweet hangin Christ, said Batman.

THEY FOUND THE WEST ARM OF the Swan River two days later, the sight of which meant the crossing through the eastern ranges was done. Fragile cloud was stretched across the sky's ribcage and the rovers spread along the riverbank filling their canteens, watching crows circle above them. They followed the whitewater for miles through a rainforest of man fern and sassafras where everything, every rock and tree and root, was shrouded in moss and every breath brought them the stink of decay. They followed the river and after descending a hill on dusk the forest dried and became the brittle gum scrub of the plains. The bark scrolls crackled once more underfoot and grass swept around their knees. Black Bill called attention to the blue trunk of a gum to which he'd pressed his hand. It was marked with another of the broad arrows. The men looked at it and then at John Batman. But he merely hefted his shotgun up on his shoulder and kept on walking. They camped on a desolate stretch of country around a fire which burned hot and clear and in its ashes roasted a damper. The party men eased back and picked their teeth with twigs as the stars arrived like snow. The pipes went around each man and they listened to Horsehead hold forth on the circumstances of his imprisonment.

You want some mashey? this fellow says. I knew his face from about the place. Knew it well. So I asks him, Are you a ganger? A ganger's a fool, he says. I says, I know you come the queer with Rolley's lot. I heard it from old man Rolley.

The boy watched him intently. You took his mashey then? he said.

Well he reveals a shillin and gives it to me. I study it in me hand. It aint even round. But the house where I drank, you see, the bitch behind the counter always had a skinful. I reckoned it probable she would take it.

Ow much you pay?

I give four shillins over and he gives twenty back.

Twenty is fair, the boy said.

Fair if you can pass them, you mean.

I could've passed them.

You might well could have. A cunnin thing like you.

Well? What did you do?

We head into town for a pot of hotegg dont we. I pay me bad shillins to this bitch and smile like I mean it. About as liquored as any woman ought to be, she was. Sodden. You never saw nothin like it. Rough old bitch too. Had all her teeth knocked out by her husband who was amiss in the head. He'd gone after this bitch with a poker one night then carried her bloody teeth into the street and told strangers he had done for her and passed them out as if they was boiled lollies. A nasty sort she was ever since and I'll attest to it.

She got you good.

She did that. I wont never forget that face when she tapped on the winderpane. We was there takin our hotegg outside when she tap tap tapped on the winder. She's callin me back. Holdin up that mashey and showin her gums. I look at young Houghton, me mate, and we just bolt. Full pelt. That might have been the end of it, you know, but God dont take warmly to me now, does he? We run, Houghton and me, but there upon the street is a constable takin a leisurely stroll and he sees us pair and his interest is raised. He produces his baton and clobbers the both of us. Just like that. We might a bin runnin for our lives for all he knew. Where's the justice in it? Course the old bitch from the taproom comes bustin around the corner, dont she. Sees the constable there. Shows him the bad shillins. He belts us again a few times until we was black about the ears and he had us in the lockup by dark.

Howell Baxter cast aside the bone he had been gnawing and he turned to Horsehead and the boy where they sat in conversation. Now here you be, in a prison with no bars.

That's it, said Horsehead. Suffering my years of it. But I done it and I'll wear it. You wont never hear me cry foul.

At that point John Batman interjected. He was standing with one leg cocked up on a stone, his thumbs hooked through his belt loops, a curved pipe set to one cheek. He plucked the pipe and jabbed it at Horsehead. The ticket's the thing, you see. Get that and yer as good as free.

The ticket. Yes. I swear on me balls when I get the damned thing that bitch will be the first to know. She'll piss her petticoats as I bowl through the door with me pistols. And her with nothin but a wet rag. She'll be sorry for it then.

The barwoman? I should have thought the constable was the cause of your sufferin. He was the one what took you.

Horsehead looked at Batman. His eyes pinched against the breeze. You what?

Seems plain as the nose on yer head. He's the one.

No. That whore spoke in the dock. She sent me here.

Aye, she spoke. But he caught you.

Howell Baxter leaned in like a conspirator as he addressed Horsehead upon the same point. I'm with Mr. Batman here, he said. How it goes the constable ought rightly to be the mark. Tis simple, given that you might otherwise be free.

Horsehead's face clouded up. His eyes darted between them and his forehead pulled into a series of deep folds. He tapped the points of his fingers together. I have never spared a thought for the constable, he said.

High time you did, said Batman. He's the wretch you want.

They were silent a moment. Jimmy Gumm was picking his teeth in the gloom and he threw the pick on the fire. He sucked at his front teeth and sat upright. Listen, he said. You cant hit a woman, can you? I mean even one what deserves it. She's still a woman, aint she?

Mate, I dont care if she's a baby in its crib, said Horsehead. She'll get it all right.

Women aint got sense enough to plan nothin. She didnt fink about it, she just acted out of her nature and that's all. But that ganger. Well. He sold you that shoddy knowin full well you would get caught. He took yer shillins and he sent you on a fool's errand, didnt he? Forget the woman. Find that man of Rolley's and show him yer pistols, my friend, and then you can sleep easy.

Horsehead threw up his painted hands. The woman, the ganger, the watchman. Am I to kill em all?

Through the murk of smoke they watched him and they all began to speak, each putting forward his own counsel.

Said Gumm: Yer a fool if you hunt that constable.

The woman spoke against you in the dock so it ought to be her, said the boy.

It is the watchman took you, said Batman, and it's him deserves your fury.

In the midst of that discussion Black Bill lifted his gaze and assessed the men from where he was seated within his blankets. When you wade into the river you muddy the water downstream, he said.

188

They watched Black Bill, frowning, but he offered nothing further on his thesis. They shook their heads or dismissed him with waves of the hand.

What's a black know, they said, of justice?

And the rovers debated on into the night the merits or otherwise of Horsehead's avengement and the means by which it might be secured, certain crooks in Liverpool he should call upon, the worthiness of wheel locks or dog locks, the superiority of various flints for ignition, ways to escape once the act was done.

After a time a quiet fell upon the campsite. Bill sat back and kicked out his boots, the pipe alight in his lips. He knew justice and it knew him.

...

Come morning the hoarfrost had rendered all the heath as white as sea salt and Bill was shivering over the campfire and blowing life into the embers. He blew until flames burst on the pile of tinder then he laced his rimed boots and struck out across the grass for a piss in the dawn light. A warm cloud of steam rose from the earth and as he was taking stock around him he saw two rows of prints trod across the frosted mud towards the plains. He buttoned up his pants and bent to study the pressings. Men and barefooted. He walked back to the camp where Pigeon's blankets were heaped upon his knapsack and

Crook's too. So they'd risen before sunrise for God only knew what reason. Bill peered after the footprints but saw nothing resembling the willowy men of the Dharug anywhere.

As the sun ascended the frost softened and the prints lost definition but still the Dharugs had not returned. Jimmy Gumm settled the billycan in the flames and the assignees scooped out mugfuls and drank while they waited for the men to show. Batman swabbed his tea with damper then sucked his fingers clean. It was another mugful each before the Dharugs made an appearance. They came ambling back, appearing in no hurry. But as they neared, Pigeon called to the campsite.

Saw smokes, he said.

John Batman scanned the skyline and there in the windless morning air stood a chimney of white.

No blacks?

None. But it's proper good fire.

Is it?

Smoke got right shape. Right colour. Them native buggers I reckon.

The green wood on their cook fire squealed and smoked damply. John Batman rubbed his heavy eyes. All right, he said, all right.

They walked to the rim of the heathland, walked through melted frost with the prison slippers dragging around their feet and only the barefoot blacks moving with ease. Shards of sharp sun jagged across the heath so that fine black shadows ran off every grass blade and the men visored their eyes onehanded as they walked, watching the smoke bend in the fresh wind. In this manner the party pushed miles east of the Swan River and into the hills before noon. Here the bush took on a different cast and they made good ground up the incline through the spindle. In the early afternoon Horsehead called for a rest.

Let's just sit here a minute, wont you? he said.

It was a request Batman had to allow as Horsehead dropped to his knees and could not be raised. Sweat ran freely from his forehead and his few squalid strings of hair stuck to his pate. The company stood their pieces together, triangled in the fashion of infantry, and they lay up on the rocks while Horsehead held his wounded hand tenderly. The Dharugs took no rest but rather kept up an audit of the sky and ground. After a moment they hurried the men to move.

Get along, get along, said Pigeon. We losem all. Lose that big chief. Get up.

Horsehead muttered into his newgrown beard and pushed Pigeon away when he tried to pull him up by the arms.

All right, I'm moving, he said.

Oldun like you got no business out here.

I aint old, you redarsed ape.

Us younguns we plenty strong enough.

I'll keep up.

What?

I said I'll keep up.

You bloody dead soon look at you.

Yeah. Well. I might be and all.

But soon they were pushing off into the foothills strung along the throat of the Swan River, illshaped gems fashioned from the fabric of the earth itself. The front-marking Dharugs led the party into the range where the mid-afternoon sun was cast over by the cloud banks assembled in the east.

At first the hills appeared slight but soon they found themselves dragging on saplings or stones to reach the blowing heights above. They rested on the peak, looking down upon the heathland, away past the Swan as the glacial wind whirred in the crevices and ransacked the dwarf gums along the cliff. The storm ran snow from the South Pole three thousand miles across the sea and as it fell the landscape faded. Bill plucked a leaf for his lips but found no comfort in the act. He took one last glance at that wounded country and tossed the thing aside.

They beat across the peak following the wallaby runs snaking through the paraffin bush and tufted grass. Storm heads formed above in a broad armada and the temperature dropped until their fingers ached in the cold.

After a time Black Bill walked out ahead of the party to scan the heavens for native smoke. The Dharug men soon joined him and the forward party paced through the alpine country as peels of snow fell soft as ash. They turned up their faces to the sky—snow caught in Crook's beard and spattered the maroon sock cap he wore, and the damp draggles of Pigeon's hair clung to his cheeks—but any sight of the native smokes had vanished. They walked through the thickening drifts and left tracks between the immature musks. The rovers came behind stepping in the holes they'd made in the snow. It was melancholy work they found there on that hillside as the storm scrubbed it over. The assigned men pleaded with Batman to make a shelter out of the weather but he held his belt pistol drawn and primed as he brought up the rear, herding those men onwards.

Before long the Parramatta men and Black Bill came upon a stone field angling away down the hillside. It was a steep piece of country denuded of trees or bushes and littered with boulders, decorated now in light snow. They looked at each other then looked back at the white men trailing some distance behind.

They wont lose us, said Bill.

You go, old man, said Pigeon. We follow you.

Crook was cradling his bare feet to warm them a little but he stood up and yanked his cap low over his ears when Bill moved off across the stones. The Vandemonian clambered several yards down the rocks and he turned to see if the Dharug men were in train but what he saw instead startled him so thoroughly that he tumbled back on the stones. A clanswoman was watching him from beneath a ledge. She was stationed there out of the weather and she held her furs to herself and frowned at the whitened world and the black man come lately upon it. He brought his gun around.

Pigeon, he called, and he pointed.

The Dharug men approached with their weapons raised before them, the stocks pressed into their waists.

Watch it. She has a waddy.

She no trouble. Are you, missus?

She did not move as the men straddled the rocks and drew up around the small cave, and she showed not the least astonishment at their presence.

Somethin wrong with her, said Pigeon.

Bill gazed around at the world rendered mute by the storm and then back at the woman. I dont see tracks leading up here. She's been sitting a while just so.

You got yourself a proper good spot here, missus.

Might be she was left behind.

I go call Batman. Pigeon climbed on top of the ledge. He waved his arms and waved his piece.

collare lueth win? Bill said to her.

Naked but for a kangaroo mantle and the pouch and strings of shells hanging at her throat, her dry breasts draped like leather stockings, her gaze as level as a marksman's, she looked up at him with changeless brown eyes. She looked right into him and he pushed back his hat, biting his lips in thought. Beside him Crook became uneasy. He shifted backwards a few halfpaces and he gestured at her chest and said something.

Black Bill leaned down and raised her mantle. It was fashioned from the fur of a white kangaroo and showed high standing among her own kind, for such skins were exceedingly rare. Beneath the mantle the skin of her torso was writ with chartings of power by means of glass or tektites or perhaps knives. Crook saw it for an omen and he scratched himself and stood further off. Black Bill cut the strap of the pouch looped at her throat and weighed it in his palm then stuffed it in his knapsack.

By now the rovers were alongside them, staring down at the woman. John Batman considered this new turn of events.

Where there's one there's fifty, he said. He bent over the woman. collare lueth win? he said.

But the woman lowered her head.

I tried that already, said Bill.

You get much?

Bout as much as you just got.

She must be sick or somethin.

Bill shook his head. She's not sick.

Might be she was waitin fer us. Just sittin here like this.

Yes, said Bill. It might be.

The snow was killing whatever hope remained of finding the source of the smokes, and the party men waited with snow trembling in their beards and the winds freezing their soaked clothes. There seemed a good amount of sense in making camp inside the stone alcove where the woman had fixed herself. Batman pulled his flask from his shirt but it was empty and he held the bottle before him as if he intended to cast it down on the stones. Instead he ordered the canvas breakwind erected. Then he pulled the cork and took a deep draught of the rum scent inside the glass.

...

The snow fell and fell. The rovers hovered near the glow of the little fire Batman had raised from his tinder but the fire cast no heat nor did it improve their nerves as would a good blaze. They shivered and could not stop. In the eerie halflight Black Bill emptied the contents of the woman's pouch into his hat and fingered through the few effects. Half a child's jawbone inset with milk teeth, a small spoon scored and tarnished, a nugget of ironglance for blacking about the eyes, and a clawshaped impactite. He took the glassy fragment and raised it before the flames. It was translucent and darkish green, serrated along one edge. He placed the impactite into the breast pocket of his shirt and the rest he scooped back into the pouch, which he returned to his knapsack. The woman stared at him. Pigeon had bound her with a woven cord and she held her hands in her lap and watched Bill at every movement.

Got a vicious set of eyes on her, dont she? said Jimmy Gumm, forgetting his own wandering eyeball.

John Batman leaned forward. Ask her again where the rest is.

Black Bill put the question to her.

The woman turned slowly and regarded the rovers and her expression grew bitter. In the long silence that followed, Bill's query went unanswered.

nina tunapri mina kani, he said.

The woman brought her peculiar gaze to bear upon him, her head turning to his as if wrenched by some unseen hand. Bill watched that inscrutable face. She put her forefinger to her cheek then pointed at him once more, a gesture of knowing, of connection. He watched and waited. Then the cleverwoman began an oratory directed at the Vandemonian alone. She called him the relentless wind at dawn and she described for him the method by which the ear might be stopped with clay to prevent his evil entering the brain. She flourished her bound hands in agitation. The scars along her arms were raised and purple in the cold. Then she proffered for the Vandemonian the notion that he had given birth to himself, disgorged whole from his own mouth as it was supposed by some. But this was a theory she did not credit for she believed him a man like all men, fed by a mother, carried by a father.

Shut that sound up, said Batman. He tapped his pipe on the midden stones around the fire.

Bill moved towards the woman with a rope in his fingers. When he caught her wrist she jerked away and continued her speechifying. The men of the roving party, caped in blankets and snow, watched him at his mishandlings.

She saw disease upon him, she said. Some devilry had passed behind his eyes or burrowed through his mouth and infected him. Now he walked that evil over her country. Shadowed under his hat, his boots blackening the pastures. She spoke and spittle gathered on her thin lips. The first notion of white men, she said, was to possess. Now Bill brought their notions into her country like a man bearing antridden firewood.

Woman, I tell you now: shut your hole, said Batman, drawing his skinning knife.

Black Bill stood over her and he forced one knee down and pinned her against the stones beneath. He looped the cord through her mouth and yoked a fiendish hitch knot behind her ear and she gagged on the bit and slaver coursed down her chin where blood also ran. They had themselves then a fine unbroken silence.

Hobbled among the rocks and drifts of snow the clever-woman lay, soundless, her mantle frosted and her eyes tracing the tumult of embers smouldering in the darkness.

THEY ROSE WITH THE SUN. OVERNIGHT the snow had ceased and the settled inch on the breakwind had started running as the temperature increased. No provisions remained for any sort of meal so they heaped snow on the fire to extinguish it completely and waited and shivered while Crook and Pigeon sought a bearing from the sun as it surged higher through the slanted ranks of trees. After some discussion Pigeon took Crook's bare foot in his hands and heaved him into the limbs of a cider gum that stretched into the canopy out of sight. Crook spidered up the branches and set them shaking and the snow lumps falling. When he'd made a decent height he turned his head to look about.

What's he see? said Batman.

Pigeon called up to him.

A reply echoed down.

He see your wife take bath, said Pigeon. See her great big tits.

Can the dirty beggar see any smokes?

Pigeon called up again and the call came down. A lake, he sees a lake.

. . .

A tract of forest banked down to the waterhole and they inched the awkward decline holding handfuls of shrubs that cut their palms. Jimmy Gumm pressed his foot to one snowshadowed fold that gave beneath him and he toppled sideways across an outcropping. Bill was the man behind him. He took grip of Gumm's clothing and dragged him upright. It was a deed simply done. After a month of bush life Gumm was all bone and beard and bitter feeling.

Bleeding treacherous, he said, a man'll kill himself.

Horsehead gripped Gumm's foot as he descended. You should hope it.

I've no desire to die on these rocks.

Better to go all sudden like that, Gummy. Save havin one of them poison spears hooked in yer breastplate.

Shut yer piehole, Horse.

The cleverwoman clambered down the rocks, pressing herself flat through the cracks and taking grip of the clefts. Bill fed out the slack on her tether and sent her first down the roughest stretches then followed the route she'd taken. She would squat and wait for him to arrive. There was a starkness about her eyes warning him never to show his back. They walked in single file through the last few gums to the water. It was some kind of natural catchment or crater and the shrunken pines about the banks grew at odd angles, clinging fistlike to the granite. Within the mire of ice and mud turned the pure planed eye of water. They followed Crook around its rim.

In the snow at the pond's shore tracks like plaster reliefs of feet ran everyway. They were sharp and the bottoms hard-packed. Crook spoke at length on what he saw there, indicating with little dips of his head where the clansfolk had descended into the gully and where, having filled the watercarriers, they continued around the waterhole and off into the woodlands. Pigeon listened and put to him questions about the nature of the clan and they conferred on the age of the tracks and the sun's influence upon their definition. Then Pigeon approached the party men.

Plenty folk. Some kids I reckon. One bugger drag foot.

How long?

Not long boss. Hour or two.

John Batman smoothed his hair back, replaced his hat. A lone currawong was turning against the sky where long blades of sunlight knifed through the cloud cover and broke open their mass.

There isnt the man alive what can hide when an inch of fresh snow is present.

No sir.

Onwards, he said. We'll havem by darkfall.

But the assigned men didn't move. They looked at each other and at Batman.

We aint got no vitals, said Horsehead. He was sleepless, pale, the ridges of his skull showing through his skin.

John Batman regarded him blankly. There is food to be had all around.

Nothin an Englishman would eat.

Just as well you aint English then.

Course I am.

No. You are Vandemonian now. My word you are.

Horsehead eyed him suspiciously. I should know what I am and what I'm not.

Batman was done talking however so he moved away towards the lip of the pond where he filled his canteen and drank and watched the black shape of the currawong repeated on the pummelled surface.

. . .

They slogged out through the scrub, stepping in those native tracks or on what bare ground they saw. The icy drifts of snow grew brittle and transparent as the day wore on and their numb feet stumbled through the slush, the few birds that still held the trees staring down upon them. They passed beneath a leatherwood where lichen platelets laddered up the trunk and the ground seemed mostly dry. They called upon Batman for a spell but he neither spoke nor spat and merely kept at the chase. They crossed a stand of pandani gathered like longhaired madwomen, snow blooms borne aloft in their axils. Crook signalled the party men onwards with his hands as he went from log to rock barefoot as a cat. He crouched atop a fallen tree and studied the crescent valley in its finery of snow. Behind him the company gathered and gazed too over that desolate country. The cleverwoman among their ranks breathed grimly around her gag and the assigned men gritted their eyes into a wind that blew ice flakes from the branches. Batman bunched his blankets around himself then called them forward into the teeth of the gale.

Further down the hill the Dharugs led them upon a fire pit strewn about with possum bones and wood spirals where spears had been carved and hardened in the flames and rounds of breadroot had been cooked. The men sniffed at the leavings then ate timidly, picking over the bones for meat skerricks. In the trodden soil around the fire Black Bill read the tracks of children pressed in perfect detail of toe and arch, his gentle fingers feeling over the imprints. Then John Batman hounded them on by waving his weathered hat and they followed the black men where they led.

...

Soon they passed out of the alpine country into a gully of fern trees that choked off the light. They descended over an hour into a rainforest dressed with species of mountain ash and man fern. At the base of a colossal candle gum Crook came to a stop. All around their thighs bracken stood as if arranged in vases and the gums and the thinner wattles of the underscrub ran aslant along the upslope. He raised his hand for silence as he studied the hillside where breaths of wind caught the treetops and stones broke the mountain snowfall. He looked and listened. The assigned men and John Batman stood deployed behind him in a line. Upon the winds they heard the humming of voices.

Batman signalled to seek cover and the men dispersed among the ferns and scrub that smothered the valley floor. They arranged themselves in silence and muffled the blow of their breaths behind their collars. The rainforest spanning the hill seemed suddenly filled with a life of its own. As they watched, some of the nearby trees began to shake and a black dog appeared on the hill, then another and a third and fourth, dark shapes against that green world. On their flanks were broken images and shapes of suns and dotted lines traced in ochre. Several of the men trained their guns on the game hounds but Batman motioned them to lower their weapons; no sooner had he done so than two bald black heads showed starkly in the foreground. They passed behind a tree but soon reappeared and the cleverwoman beside Black Bill tried to call around her gag until the Vandemonian caught her throat and cut off the air. The native women were carrying firesticks. Bill saw only two but reckoned a further three from the scrub by their firestick smoke. The two women neared, scrabbling down a bank of mossy rocks, the children they lugged on their backs sitting small in their grey fur slings.

Hold now, whispered John Batman.

Among the group of five women now appearing from the trees were a pair of young warrior boys. The foremost boy was bare naked but for a huge corduroy jacket that hung off his bones like fool's costuming. He jostled the other with his bony elbow and seemed to be retelling some hunting story as he raised his thin spear and mimicked a throw then elbowed his mate again.

Black Bill kept his neck lock on the old woman. Her breath drew woundedly as the dogs trotted within yards of the hidden rovers and put their noses to the air. John Batman, holding his hat, looked up and down the ranks of fellows concealed in the brush and motioned them to lay aside their arms. At first they were confounded by this but he made the gesture again and the assigned men put down their guns and knapsacks. Then without warning Batman lunged out of the underbrush. He rose to full stature like the fabled barbarian all garbed in wool bedding and bearded and the sight put the dogs into a frenzy. From beneath his blankets he levelled his belt pistol on one and fired and its skull shattered in a spray as if a bottle of claret had been dashed against the cobbles. The whole of that native body cried out at his appearance: wa wa wa! they called but he was already among them, grabbing at the nearest woman.

Following his example the assigned men circled about and took hold of the women and their tots together and wrestled them to the ground. The young warrior boys brought up the blackened points of their spears but Bill caught the first spear when it was thrust and disarmed the boy. As the second spear pierced Bill's shirt folds he twisted and seized it also with his free hand and likewise tore it from the youth's fingers. Both spears he then broke in his hands. Gumm cracked one boy viciously across the face, bloodying his nose and dropping him cold.

The women rubbed their cheeks in shock, the little ones slung upon their backs wide eyed and staring. Gould looped a length of cowhide cord around the women's hands and feet and some of them lowered their heads and cried out and made gestures of horror while others called out their shame with sounds most pitiful to hear. Their miserable cacophony filled the gully and John Batman paced before the captives, striking them about the head to regain some silence, and they cowered and wept and fell quiet.

Where are the men? John Batman scrutinised the man ferns and the sunless dells all around. Where's the headman?

The faces of the clansfolk were lowered but their eyes cut towards Batman as he seated a shot ball in the breach of his pistol. Batman turned to regard that mob. bungana? he said. bungana?

Please, no men. One of the women raised her head. No men,

no men, she intoned in a weird echo of the whites. She carried no child on her back, and her skin was lighter than the others.

Stand her up, said Batman.

Bill picked her up by the arms.

Cranking back the cock, Batman placed the gun to her temple. Bill angled his face away from the blast but Batman only held the weapon steady. Held it close enough that she might study the patterned engraving upon the forestock.

You call em in, he said.

The woman stared along the barrels at Batman's blank face and whatever she saw therein convinced her of his cold intent. She called into the unkept land that ran down the valley, her cry played away and died. She waited then called again.

Tell that chief I am here for him. John Batman spoke evenly.

Eh?

carney Manalargena, he said.

The woman turned and looked out at the forest. She seemed unsure whether anything she might say could summon the headman and she looked at the forest and then back at her captors. Batman put his hand to his mouth in a motion of yelling. So the woman raised her hands reluctantly and copied him. A small sound gone upon the air and lost. There came no reply.

John Batman looked over the row of blacks, hands and feet made fast. They were caped in the thick winter pelts of mountain wallaby. Spindly-boned and now harrowed of heart and soul in their aggregate. A child wandered among them, her rib bones as plain as ship's strakes. He looked them over then reset the hammer on his pistol.

Gumm, he said.

Jimmy Gumm put down the rope he was holding.

Take yer piece. Take Baxter there and Horsehead. Go see about the men.

Gumm glanced around at the others and then back to Batman. Just us three? he said.

Three'll do it.

Like hell it will.

Batman brought up his pistol.

Aye and you can shoot me. It's better than what I'll get from them blackfolk if I goes out there.

They stood like that through a few moments, Batman with his pistol upheld and Gumm mightily unsettled. Then Batman lowered his weapon. He turned instead towards Pigeon, who was squatting with Crook in the shrubs, sharing some breadfruit taken from the women. They would not look at Batman. They chewed and wiped their mouths but they would not face him.

Youse are all gone to water, he said and he holstered his pistol. The lot ayou.

Then the Vandemonian stepped from the recessed shadows. He came forward with his fowling piece crosswise behind his neck. I'll go, he said, and began to walk into the swath of rainforest funnelling away down the valley.

Batman spat on the dirt. He ran his eye across the rovers waiting there before him. Gone to water, he said and shook his head.

He was turning to follow Bill when a great spear flashed in flight from the trees, burying half its length in the damp earth at Batman's feet where it stood ticking side to side. He stepped back. The spear was ten foot at least and as thinshafted as an arrow. He looked around at Bill who was similarly studying the weapon.

Batman cried out into the forest. Manalargena, he said. puguleena toomla pawa.

But it was just one spear that came. A single charred haft raised among the glades and stones of that place. They scanned the spread of gums and the thick understorey where it trailed away before them. Tangles of creeping heath hung from the branches and wavered in the wind. They watched but there were no clansmen to be seen. It was as if the haft had fallen from the snow clouds. All the while the women cried.

You make any? said Batman.

Bill scanned here and there. All I see is bush.

Well seems they can see us sure enough.

They're out there some place.

I dont see nothin, said Horsehead.

Be quiet a minute.

Above the moaning from the clanswomen could be heard another, more sinister sound. They listened, each man of that company, to a sound as of tigerwolves yowling. The war cry of the forest people.

Christ, you hear that?

What'll we do?

Bring em with us, said Batman.

The trussed blacks were strung along a single rope all despairing, calling intermittently to the menfolk concealed nearby. There came no such call in reply however. The assignees found themselves some starters for chasing up the lazy and they hit at the prisoners with them and cursed them as cannibals or worse, whatever was needed to get them along. The party retraced their path up towards the mountain country they'd so recently quit and John Batman stood by, holding his doublebarrel gun and studying the clutch of scrub from where the spear had dropped. Then he turned to follow the women.

. . .

They drove the women and children and boys up the valley before them. There was about the clanspeople a burdensome misery that put lead in their bones and but for some floggings they would not be moved at all. As they hiked into the hill country Batman brought up the rear, walking with his gun at his waist and searching the back trail for sign of the men. A wind stirred the bush into life and Batman saw everywhere new movements which from time to time caused him to raise his gun and fire. At that sound the women would cry out in anguish.

We shall be made to earn this yet, he said to Bill.

A host of game dogs followed at a distance. They crowded together in padding up the foreslope or out among the bracken with their obscene tongues flailing through their teeth. Across the afternoon as the company ascended into the hills and pushed onwards for the Swan River John Batman set to trimming their numbers, until there was left strewn along the trail a mix of the dead and dying, the wounded dragging their entrails, whining, licking at themselves. He finished some of them beneath his boot heel but others he left half alive on the wayside where they made a gruesome caveat for those clansmen following in pursuit. Soon the roving party approached a flat hilltop and crossed under the snow gums so prominent where the ground was stony. The captives no longer struggled but grew dour and resigned themselves to walking so that in time the men threw aside their switches and merely walked with them.

Late in the day they took a spell on a stretch of sedge land, crouching in the button grass out of the weather. During that halt Batman brought the black men together but for what purpose he would not say. They'd come west across the flat and their path through the grass could be seen stretching back a mile or more; Batman squatted beside them in the growth and looked from one to the next. They watched as he called attention to the country with a sweep of his arm and then he turned momentarily to assess it himself as the wind swell laid the brown fields over and disturbed all the bushes.

There is high ground off thataways, he said.

You see em? Pigeon said.

I dont need to. They're comin.

Black Bill scratched his whiskered chin. Then he stood and looped his knapsack over his head and retrieved his tall weapon.

Watch for us at nightfall, he said.

The wind caught at his hat and he tugged it low over his forehead. He pushed out through the pasture with his shirt billowing and the Dharug men gathered up their effects and put out behind him. As the black men passed, the captives renewed their mournful calling, the tugging of the cheeks and hair, the smearing of dirt upon skin, straining against their bound hands for they understood the rearguard's grim intent. The three black men walked with their firearms rattling across their backs and the cries of the clanspeople fading.

. . .

They found some cover on an overlook which allowed a view across the neatly scrubbed plain. The tufts of trees were regular across it all and the wide trail the company had made in their procession snaked through the grass. A line of smooth rock ran the width of the hill and they sheltered behind this and out of sight. Not much remained of sunshine. As the shadows lengthened on the grasslands the black men looked over that discoloured world and waited. Bill produced his makings and packed a pipe from his pouch. He dragged a spark off the stones with his knife and into a wad of dry tinder, pressed the small flame to the bowl and drew back. They shared it as was their habit. And in that familiar action they found some comfort.

The first of the dark figures emerged from the trees upon dusk. He stood and gazed out across the flat. Then two more appeared, and another two. In the fading sunlight the menfolk looked pieced from the waste of the frontier, garbed in skins and bits of battered clothing and painted up for war. Soon ten men stood grouped upon the plain. They formed up and made forward along the company's trail, walking with the aid of their spears. At the head of that assemblage was Manalargena and all the men seemed pulled along in his wake as they forded the deep grasses in pursuit of the roving party. From their concealment the rovers looked along their ironsights at that ragged band.

The first shot rang out in the twilight. One clansman pitched backwards, splayed out in the grasses where he lay clutching his bloodied shoulder. Crook repacked his rifle from the powder bag and watched as the clansmen came nervously around the fellow. Some of them gazed about in confusion looking for the shooters. From the barrel it was a distance best measured in furlongs yet Crook figured the wind against his aim and then fired again. Another man fell but promptly stood again, grasping at the hole in his arm. Several of their number pointed towards the stony hillside and when the three rovers moved from cover bearing their levelled pieces a collective roar went up that signalled the clansmen's terror and bravery in equal measure.

warlipare warlipare warlipare!

Spears came hurling in from throws of fifty yards and the thin shafts skittered on the rocks or sank into the earth. The rovers held back a moment until the volley ceased and then continued swiftly down the hill. The menfolk made a general retreat now and as he walked down the slope Crook fired at their backs. One of the clansmen tumbled and fell, hauling himself through the grass, and his brothers dropped their heads and bolted for the trees. Only one man was left striding up the hill towards the injured man. The headman, fiercely howling, launched his blackwood waddy, sent it spinning end over end, until it clattered off the stones at Crook's feet. The shot clansman struggled to his feet but Manalargena was with him and caught up his arms.

The rovers jogged back within weapons range and brought up their guns and knelt to steady themselves. They fired at the headman, flame tongues flashing in the halfdark. He had draped the fallen warrior across his shoulder and the clansman cried out as the shot balls bit his flanks but the headman kept walking through the low grass as if at leisure. The rovers repacked. For a time there was only the sound of their tamping, the sliding of rod along hollow iron. By now Manalargena had re-entered the trees and when they stood to fire he was nowhere to be seen. They scanned the weave of alpine scrub along their sights. To follow him into that realm was a near thing to suicide. Bill looked about at the Dharugs but there was no appetite for the chase written upon their faces. So he slung his firearm and wheeled away from the trees.

The dead man lay staring up at the sky. A hole was punched through him which revealed his ruptured rib bones and another hole in his neck bled darkly on the grass. Bill studied the trees where the clansfolk had vanished for a moment before he knelt beside the body. The man was shaven clean about the cheeks, young of face and build, and ochred in the patterns of his clansmanship. He was suited up in verminous canvas breeches and hung about with a wallaby pelt secured by means of a chewed leather string. When Bill turned out the fellow's pockets he found a handful of throwing stones for birding but nothing by way of food.

Bill stood up.

That's enough, he said.

And so the three men returned along the company's trail, alone now upon that plain.

...

On nightfall the menfolk returned to the flats, abandoning their cover to gather around the body. Manalargena called to him and the others also spoke his name. They pulled him upright but the fellow was long dead and he slumped over soundlessly. The land lay wholly in shadow now and the men in the sinking dark sat beside their kinsman and held his cold hands. A fresh snowfall began upon them but they neither moved nor looked up.

THE TRIO WALKED THROUGH THE WOODS down to the plains before the Swan River where a signal fire burned. It glowed on the flat lands like the gateway to some infernal realm and led them onwards until, much used up by the trek, they found camp. One of the clan dogs was hung on skewers over the flames. It had been roughly skinned but the head and feet remained and its teeth were bared in a strange petrified grin. Some meat was passed to them and it was thoroughly blackened and speckled with sandy ash. They ate and Batman put his questions to them.

You see them off?

We did.

A sorrier bunch of crows I never knew.

Bill pulled dog hair from his mouth. He chewed the black and fibrous meat around and tried to swallow. They wont catch us, he said.

They couldnt catch clap in a cat house. Batman tossed his tea dregs on the fire.

The night lay heavy upon them. But for the dim flare of the coals as the wind worked through the campsite there was no light at all and Black Bill slept uneasily. He woke once and sat upright in his blankets. The two remaining native dogs fought over the offal from their gutted comrade, snatching at each other or snarling, until Bill stood, kicked one dog in the rump, sending it skittering, and both scattered into the darkness. When he turned back the cleverwoman was staring at him. She was perched like a black abomination near the coal glow and the shells at her throat chattered as she raised her jowled arms towards the sky.

She said the moon sat wrongly.

Bill looked up but there was nothing beyond the press of limbs and leaves, nothing but the night itself.

weeta mayangti byeack, he said.

She told him to look again and when he gazed upwards the cloud cover dispersed and there was a ponderous moon as white as the rolling eye of a convulsive. Black Bill studied the awful sight then turned his face away. The cleverwoman whispered something through the darkness but he was not listening. He lowered himself onto his bedding and gathered the blankets around his shoulders. The cleverwoman continued to whisper. She claimed that Manalargena was conjuring beneath this moon and his retribution would be proffered blind and bloodslicked like the battles of old. She held up her own bound hands as if to show how that act might be done. Bill lowered his hat over his eyes and in that unspoiled darkness his mind worked upon the image of a woman and her swollen belly and his own hand placed on her. He huddled there and kept his thoughts ever enclosed. Soon the cleverwoman fell silent.

In the night his unborn son found him as he sometimes had. Bill carried him through a stand of fired sassafras and all about was blackened and the burnt ground shattered as he trod it. They moved between the killed trees and into a clearing, father and son. At the centre of the burn stood a black gibbet and from the noose swung a body. A charred body, its white eyes open. Bill placed the boy down on that cauterised country and the child looked up at the gently swaying corpse. Who is it? he said.

But Bill was gone rigid with grief.

THE FOLLOWING MORNING WAS COLD IN the shadowed trenches of those back hills, cold enough to quiet the bird call and quiet the captives as well. But they slogged on and by midday had reached Brushy River. It was muddied with meltings from the snows and it seeped down the valley through the wooded hills like the discharge from some sore on the planet's crust. As they tracked along the banks squalls of mosquitoes lit on their bare skin, broad things the size of Spanish dollars, and the assignees beat at themselves with long switches of gum to drive them away. The clansfolk shuffled along clinging each to the other, mothers to children, sisters to sisters, and only the young warrior boys watched the white men, but they did so out of fear. For two days Jimmy Gumm had been carrying a child, a girl round of cheek and belly. During the spells he passed the child back to its mother and when they moved out he hauled it once more onto his back. The child did not grin or show any enjoyment but nonetheless Gumm persisted in befriending the little girl and seemed to derive some sort of satisfaction from caring for her. The next morning from a hill's crown they saw the crenellated mountains away north lying sunlit under snows with the mythic blue of Ben Lomond looming above them all. Thus the distance home was laid out before the party men.

On the morning of their fourth day of walking, the disordered party gazed across a vast plain and saw in the dawn the hamlet of Campbell Town clustered around the green row of river trees that wound through it. There was no wind to speak of, no clouds, so that the chimney smoke tracked straight up into the sky. Among the stubbled wheatfields wandered sheep in flocks and some early risers were seen to move along the cart roads. The assigned men wiped their noses and smoothed down their matted hair as best they might and the party set out towards the settlement and their first civilisation in a month.

They entered Campbell Town by noon. Folk stood in their doorways staring as the nine of the roving party moved the captives along the main street. A load of turds tossed from a night bucket reeked on the road ahead. At Batman's command the rovers circled around the captives and held their firearms readied. They stepped over the ruts and watched the wary townsfolk pick up their children and spit in the direction of the blacks, but after the party passed the townsfolk formed to the rear and followed them down the roadway. A number of public houses lined the main street, squalid huts ruinous and wrongly aligned and clad with palings cut from whatever grew at the riverbanks. Raw timber slabs were stood upon sawhorses to function as bars and the drinkers wheezed over their rum and made the sign of finger and circle at the black women. One toothless old fellow tottered forward and thanked the party men for ridding those parts of babyeaters. He shook their hands one by one, the paddock dirt still black upon his own. When he reached Bill he looked up into that hardened face and his eyes opened wide.

We'll be paid. No need for thankin. John Batman moved the fellow aside with his forestock. Then some of the children began to peg rocks at the clansfolk. They called obscenities and gave names to the blacks even Bill had never heard.

We'll have us some nice black shoes, said one, when they's tanned up this lot.

His hair was cut high around his ears and his young teeth were already yellowed but in truth every child in that group was as wretched and wild as the rovers themselves. They dashed in with sticks and stabbed at the warrior boys. Pigeon caught one by the shirt and shook him viciously then cuffed him around the ears, and the rest of the children hung back after that but they called and sang their crude songs just the same.

The only stone building on the high street was the gaol. Its squared fronting rested along a section of cobble and the assigned men stood in the street before the place they'd so freshly quit and they muttered under their breath and spat. A set of wooden double doors stood ajar and through the crack was heard the rough hacking of the inmates. An evil stink of disinfecting vinegar hung upon the whole place. John Batman brought the party up before the doorway. He straightened his wide-brimmed hat and his coat and took himself inside the doors, his boots clapping away over the flagstones as he disappeared. The rovers gripped their weapons while the people in the street gathered to watch the unfolding of events. They clamoured about as if some medicine show had pitched its tent and promised acts of miracle. Batman re-emerged bearing his hat in his hand. He was accompanied by Sergeant Bickle who, on seeing the mob of captives, twitched his moustache and stood off as if they were diseased. The clansfolk gazed on him with near identical disdain.

You've gone and done it, he said. By God you have.

He called inside the double doors and two more soldiers in misused livery stepped onto the street. They stared at the women's bare breasts.

Bickle wiped his sweaty neck. How many you got?

Eleven.

Eleven. Well I'll be damned. He waved at the lockup, a gesture of dismissal. I aint got nowheres to keep that many.

I'm contracted to collar the bastards, said Batman, or shoot them. So as you can see, Sergeant, my part is played. Their lodgings dont much concern me.

Plenty round here would see the mongrels hang, said Bickle.

Batman looked at him. Then hang em.

The gathered crowd roared in approval.

They aint worth a length of rope, cried one.

Said another: We burn heathens, dont we?

They ought to be speared just how they speared Mrs. Gough and her tots.

The sergeant clapped his hands and appealed for quiet and the protests died away. They'll be fed. More than that I cant swear to.

Protests began afresh but he signalled the guardsmen to lead the captive clansfolk into the gaol's wooden maw, the children gripping the women's cloak flaps as they went and the warrior boys straight-backed and meeting the eyes of all. At the doorway leaning on his weapon was Black Bill and as the clan filed past him, each in turn stared into his dark face, seeking some show of solidarity, some inkling that their fate lay with him, but the Vandemonian bent his head and would not look. He stared down at his boots, split open at the toe and caked with street crud, exuding a fierce stench. He stared down even as the door squealed shut on its hinges and the clansfolk vanished from sight.

Bill turned up his thick collar—there was an edge of snow on the breeze—and lowered the brim of his hat and put forth along the road alone. John Batman called his name, the name given to him by James Cox, Esquire. The boy called it too but the Vandemonian walked and ignored their cries. He walked and the townsfolk parted around him.

BEREFT OF THEIR WOMEN AND CHILDREN the clansmen crossed their clanhold at pace and progressed along the frontier as if they were as insubstantial as the stays of mistfilled light between the silver wattles. After them came the rovers, unhindered by their roped prisoners and full of their own success. The rovers traced them over shale and peat land and plain, heard of them spied atop a certain hill or camped on a certain riverbank. They walked the sun up and down eating what they shot and sleeping on the bare granite. Spring snows, a foot deep in the back hills, slowed their pursuit but they did not relent. Late October they came upon some little mia mia contrived out of broken branches and stocked with looted blankets and clothes. In the hearth pits were dead fires kindled from books torn savagely apart. The party men took rum against the frostbite, relit the native fires and slept in the native shelters. In the following days a great tail of smoke led the rovers to the corpse of a young stockhand smouldering in a hut which had been razed around him. His body black bones but his head oddly intact. His two boiled eyes steaming in the cold. They kicked through the ashes for things of worth and Batman lifted the lock of a gun with a stick and studied the redhot iron. The stockhand had made a stand inside his shelter until the bark roof was set alight by brands; no doubt he recognised a worse fate than burning awaited outside, yet no blood and no dead blacks were to be found in the underbrush. The assignees grubbed out a shallow hole in the ground into which the stockhand's bones and his roasted head were thrown and they raised a little cairn upon the grave mound so that the devils might be kept off the corpse. From that place they trailed the war party around Ben Lomond. It was a mob of at least twenty they were hunting, warrior men, youths, a meeting of broken bands come together before a foe that ran them without halt. Lately the weather had begun to advance and the spring coolness changed to an unmuzzled heat. With this the bush also altered as the trees grew brittle and the parched leaves rattled in the desert-driven northerlies. It was here, amid the rows of blue gums and acacias dried by the elements, that the war party crossed their tracks and cut back behind their pursuers. The Dharug men lay on the ground reading the faint signs pressed into the earth and they tested the depressions by finger but the deception was only understood when the blue gums along their back track flared alight like matchsticks. In all directions towers of smoke began to rise and the rovers saw there their fate. They bolted up the slope as the conflagration drew the wind inwards and climbed until they found sanctuary on a ridge. That night the underbelly of the clouds burned orange and showed the rolling front of flame and the smouldering star points in its wake. They stared at the bushfire and held their empty bellies till dawn. Come morning they walked down through the burn, their clothes blackened and their feet blistering through the skin shoes. There was nothing but devastation in all directions and even Bill knew not where to lead them in a land become suddenly alien. From there on they passed days and nights in search of the clansmen's trail. They crossed and recrossed the same cuts of country. Saw the same shepherds working the same beasts. And as the heat of summer peaked and the days began to shorten the inescapable truth presented ever more insistently. They found themselves one morning crouched over ochre diggings weeks old and collapsed under the rains and no heading could be taken nor sign discovered. John Batman looked up to the sky as rain came anew and in that moment his resolve shifted. He looked to his men, shook his head and walked away from the diggings. They passed a hard night billeted among the lime ferns and prickly box but soon after he led them homewards, goading them on like cattle when they tired. Some days later they spilled from the forest onto the cleared ground of Kingston and for a few beatings of their scabbed hearts they were satisfied, even the Vandemonian. That night Batman made free with his rum and the men drank. William Gould produced a piccolo upon which he played over and over the same sad song and the men danced at first but soon took a seasoning at the rum keg and slipped into a sullen stupor. The fire burned low and as the men passed out one by one, Black Bill was left to drape blankets on them and watch another dawn disfigure the treeline.

. . .

Sometime later Eliza shook him awake. He was lying backed against the store shed in the sunshine and on instinct he pulled his knife and raised it. Her hard eyes searched him over as he sat upright, straightened his hat and sheathed his blade. The pockmarks in her tanned cheeks stretched and shifted as she spoke.

You best see yerself home, Bill, she said, those green eyes lingering on him. Yer wife has need ayou.

Yes mam, he said. He stood up.

As he picked his way among the unconscious assignees lying on the ground he passed by the boy, who opened his eyes and rolled over. Bill continued on for the fields but the boy called to him.

Where you off to? he said.

Bill looked around. Back home.

You dont got one.

I got one. He pointed out the knot of shaded scrub beyond the sheep fields. Out bush there.

In the bush?

Yes.

Like them blacks back there?

No, not like them. I got a humpy. Got a woman.

Can I see it someday?

Anytime, boy.

Batman wont allow it, will he?

Bill shrugged. Who knows what that man will do?

Are we to be given tickets now?

That there is the Governor's business. He does as he sees fit but were I him I would see my way to it.

The boy drew his knees up. Take care of yerself.

Yes, boy. And you too.

He took the track through the scrub to his humpy at a jog. The shadows dappled in a weave patterning his skin, his booted feet slapped the earth and his fowler clattered on its securements. Long before he made the hut he smelt a smoke tang on the air and he saw the column of it rising white and crimped and brittle through the canopy. Soon he entered the clearing he'd cut by axe and shovel in the middle of that bush gully. Hearing his noise, Katherine appeared in the doorway in a disheveled pinafore and she bore in one hand a smallmouthed pistol of the kind favoured by gamblers and charlatans. She stared at him. The weapon was on the cock.

Missus, if you shoot some fellow with that little thing and he finds out, by God he will come back and flog you, Bill said and he laughed.

But his woman disappeared inside. He looked over the gums pressing in on all sides and he dropped his kit by the door, following her in. She cut strips of mutton onto a plate and placed it before him at the table where his mug filled with river water was also put down. In the smoky light Katherine appeared much aged and hard done by. The months alone had done her no favours.

Where'd the pistol come from?

I trade. Rifle too big.

Too big. Yes, I reckon it was.

Bill's woman bent down to the fire with her legs splayed outwards to permit the swell of her belly and her knees made a stretched leather groan under the load. He ate meat with his fingers and watched her set logs in the fireplace, the flames licking around her fingers. Then she turned to face him, eyes pinched against the smoke.

You find that bungana? she said.

No. He has some cunning in him.

The fire popped. She watched him a moment longer, intently, then went back to the wood and reaching flames.

DAYS PASSED WHERE THE FOREST IN all its dead summer heat reso-
nated with cicada song but Bill could not be still. He crossed
the fragrant gullies and hills searching the sky for smoke.
He shot possums and wallabies and in those lonely back-
woods he catalogued every place a man might prosecute an
ambush. He knew the likely approach routes to his shack
too, stepping out distances and firing test shots at a roo skin
propped on a branch until he had his range from all parts.
Mornings he went ahead of his woman as she walked the
miles to Batman's house into a sun that cast long stabs of
yellow through the trees, and evenings he waited for her at
the forest edge where she came carrying what few rations
Batman had allowed for her day's work and together they
returned to the shack.

This particular afternoon as he waited for his woman on
the fringe of Batman's cleared land he read the weather in the
flight of certain birds he knew and he understood the heat

would break. And so it did. When the sky split open sometime that night the rain battered the roof and water seeped through the shingles and turned the dirt floor to mud and dampened their bedding. As they lay listening, Katherine kicked out her legs. She moaned and rolled. Bill turned to study her.

Are you sick? he said but she said nothing.

The rain bore down and she writhed on the bed, her groans guttural and her breath ragged. He huddled down for sleep that never came and sometime near midnight he climbed from the bed of possum skins to stand over her.

I'll fetch Mrs. Batman, he said.

Stay, stay, she said. She was breathless.

He crouched beside the bed, the sound of the rain deafening him.

...

He held her hand and she howled, throwing back her head as if she was a penny girl having her throat cut. In the quiet moments he felt between her legs for signs before the screaming came again and she struggled anew on the sweatslicked rugs. When in time he could see her outlined on the bed in the first blush of sun the head was coming through and he knelt and received the child where it was birthed. It made no sound but squirmed and contorted as he held it nearer the light and appraised the thing in its first few moments. It was glossy like a carcass peeled of skin. The head was mishapen and lurid welts showed where eyes should have moved.

Give me, she panted.

But he did not.

Give me, she said and pushed herself upright.

The child's features, the neck and the veined head, were run together in one lumpen misconception. Bill clenched his teeth.

Give me here.

He drew his knife, severed the cord and swaddled his child, his son, with a soft wallaby skin Katherine had readied. Then he passed her the bundle. Nothing needed to be said. She cradled the child as it drew the only breaths of its short life and she watched it claw its face in pain and soon it ceased moving. Bill relieved her of it. Katherine clutched her belly and she began to cry. Her throat was hoarse and her woe was queerly muted. She huddled on the bed and cried as if she had lost everything in this world and the next.

. . .

He carried the dead child outside into the wet as the first slate shades of dawn towered above and laid the tiny bundle on the mud. In the near dark he fetched up some firewood and erected a pyre of stones and branches in rough accordance with the Panninher ritual, this custom almost lost to him. Onto the firewood he poured a flask of Batman's rum kept over from his rations. Then he laid the wrapped body of his son among the sticks and lit the blaze with a brand taken from his hearth, moving back to watch the smoke funnel towards the boiling grey sky. As the body was consumed Bill tried to sing those old dirges he'd once known but they were gone from his memory. Instead he sat upon the stones, bearing witness to this time.

The vague sun tracked unmarked across the gloom. Black Bill stayed long by that fire staring at the flames while the sky sagged. Katherine wept on her bloodied skins yet he remained impassive. A likeness of a man carved in cold black marble. All he felt was the pain. The pitiless certainty of this death. He weighed a length of wood in his hand and poked at the coals with it and by the time night had fallen again on the forest he knew this evil was the headman's doings. He gripped the wood and pondered on his redress.

...

On the morning of the following day Bill stood on John Batman's verandah looking everywhere but at him as the man ranted about the new laws the Governor had passed, laws that protected blacks beyond the settled districts. Their bounty hunting was at an end. Manalargena was known to be sojourning on the east coast beyond the frontier where settlements encroached upon his homelands and in a place where food was readily come by. In those parts he still had domain and he did not run or hide but led his band in the habits of old. But the rovers couldn't hunt him. Batman folded his arms and spat off the deck. His native boy, Ben, was squatting in front of the house and Batman and Black Bill watched the child drag his fingers through the mire and take handfuls of it for throwing. He was crouched between his knees, his short pants and shirt ballooning like a nightdress.

Bill cleared his throat. My boy died. The Vandemonian looked out across the paddocks. He come out all wrong. I reckon he died of it.

His old friend inclined his head slightly then looked away. Tis the nature of things, he said.

Batman had lost a child once, a son. He was buried in an unmarked hole and spoken of never more. The mound of dirt had been dug up by the devils soon after and the tiny foetid boy devoured but Batman had put his men to refilling the hole and straightening out the little stones before Eliza saw those desecrations. She remained unknowing even now. Batman stepped down and caught up the native boy in his hands. He carried him up to the Vandemonian and offered him over. Bill looked at the boy and he looked at Batman. Then he took the boy against his chest and kept him there just so as they spoke about farm business. Talk that Bill had no mind for as he cradled the boy and thought long on the headman.

...

Bill returned through the bush from Kingston with small sacks of flour, tea and tobacco in his pocket and a weight of mutton across his shoulder. It was generous. He knew Batman would not have given so much but for the misfortune. By now the pyre was gone cold. He dropped the stores beside his shack and walked over to pick through the ashes for pieces of bone. He found the skull and a reedy thigh bone and using handfuls of sand and water he rubbed the pieces over until the charcoal was polished away. The white beneath glistened. In the doorway Katherine sat holding her belly and watching him at his work. When the bones were clean she placed them in her palm, little shards of porcelain shattered in the heat. Clutching those bones she gazed across the entanglement of bush running down the gully as if she thought to see some wild apparition working its ruin upon her again. But there were only the trees, robed in their long shadows. She gripped the skull and stared.

...

The following day Katherine was splitting wood and fetching up water in the dress she'd worn for months: ragged, yellowed, disintegrating, and now stained with afterbirth. Bill removed his hat and from a wooden bowl kept for the purpose he fingered out some animal fat and smeared it across his face, following the line of his jaw. He stropped his knife a few times against the heel of his boot then shaved his chin and throat. He wiped the blade on a gum leaf and made another stroke. Katherine placed a bucket of water before him that he might check his reflection and wandered off inside but he called to her, his voice enormous in the clearing.

I mean to find him, he said.

She reappeared in the doorway.

Find him and be done.

At her neck was strung the child's skull on a woollen cord and she closed her hand around it.

He looked at her. I'm leaving at dawn, he said.

I come, she said. I help.

No. You cant barely walk.

I can walk.

No.

Katherine stepped inside and was gone a moment before she stood again in the sunlight showing her pistol. With her free hand she palmed back the hammer.

Before he could speak she aimed down at his feet and fired. Bill dropped the shaving knife and skipped back as the dirt blossomed. The emptied gun hung quietly between them and he moved over and took it from her hand. She looked him cleanly in the eye.

You sleep I cut your throat, she said. You walk away I shoot your back. You take me. You take me or you be killed.

He slipped the pistol into his pocket. Then he looked out across the stumps and the bracken growing in the cleared spaces around the shack. Better get some decent walking clothes at least then. A blanket. A drum.

Katherine didn't answer. She stood there in her tattered dress and her hand went again to the skull. Then she turned away and stepped into the humpy where the sound of her movements drifted to him through the cracks in the bark walls. Bill retrieved his knife and once more set to working the sharp edge along his cheek. He flicked the scum off the blade and taking another glob of possum grease smeared it over his scalp. With the knife set on an angle he began to shave the hair away. Inside he could hear her throwing things, the chair, mugs, and he stopped to listen for moment then shook his head and went about his shaving again.

...

They awoke with the birds and put forth in the dark before dawn. With them they carried neither flour nor mutton, flint nor tinder. Bill rolled a heap of embers in damp bark for a firestick and slung his fowling piece across his shoulder. He filled his powder flask, loaded his pockets with ball. That was all he needed. Katherine kitted herself up in his spare dunga-rees which she rolled at the ankle and hitched the waist with cord, and as she walked the hems scuffed along the ground.

The two of them made towards the dawn's flameglow where it bloomed beyond the hills. As they moved into the forest a miserable rain began and where it fell the bark litter darkened and the pungency of wood rot grew; the rain accompanied them that long day as they walked the unburnt back country of the Plindermairhemener. In the afternoon they crossed pastures where saplings and wild grasses stood so profuse that the grazing wallabies were hid entirely and their small furred heads rose and fell above the level as the herds bounded away. Bill checked his trail and saw his woman coming some yards behind, the grim line of her jaw unchanged and her hair and clothes speckled with grass seed. He waited while she approached and together they pushed on.

The night sky cleared as they settled their first camp at the rim of one such pasture with the wild stars already above giving light. Bill shot a native hen which they plucked and roasted and ate in silence. When it was fully dark an emerald rippling unfurled across the sky like the underside of a wave breaking upon the bladed shore of stars. They watched the aurora for a long while but they knew not how to read it. The Vandemonian took up his dagger and sharpstone and Katherine heaped up the fire. She stretched out for sleep beneath her skins and Bill sat with his back to the blaze grinding his knife with the stone, watching the jade-coloured glare in the sky manifest along the mirrored span of steel.

...

They trekked days through the hills east of Ben Lomond without sight or sound of another soul. They ate possum taken from the gum trees or little lunna bunna the shape of kidney potatoes or fern roots which they dug up with a stick. They found bush cherries. Pigface. Mushrooms where it was damp. On the fifth day they happened upon a rivulet bedded with small pebbles that Bill fingered through for some quartz pieces with which to strike fire. At dusk they found high ground and watched the sun melt at the fringe of the world. They scanned the blue-grey landscape for pinpoints of fires, only lighting their own when Bill was satisfied there burned no other. Through those days they shared few words so it surprised Black Bill when one night Katherine looked him in the eye.

Her name Kittawa, she said.

Bill was picking over some possum bones and he set them aside. He picked his teeth. Who? he said.

Katherine clutched the skull bound at her throat. As if nothing further needed saying.

He shook his head.

She need name. I call her Kittawa. Now she rest.

It was a boy.

Eh?

You heard me.

Katherine's mouth drew into a grim line. pudeyar, she said. lobudenday.

Woman, I tell you it was a boy. I got eyes in my head and I know what I saw.

She went quiet now. Her fingers felt around the cranial separations and the toothless jaws then she lowered her eyes. Bill laid the meat bones across his lap and continued picking flesh from the joints, the crevices.

. . .

With the morning's first blue gradations Bill perched on the ridge to study the country below. A tableland patterned into clearings by curving tree formations, the meadows like missing puzzle pieces. Away on the far side of one field burned a fire and that smoke was the only sign of life he'd seen in a week. It was a mile or more distant but as thick and threatening as the fires lit by whole companies of men. He shook Katherine awake by her shoulder and they ate a breakfast of cold meat, sharing water from the canteen. A few embers remained among the hearthstones so he wrapped them inside bark and tied it with grass. As he was crouched there at the fire pit he looked at her face, drawn and dulled. Bill retrieved his fowling piece and he called for her to follow him down the slope.

They walked the verge of a grassed basin, keeping to the trees and looking over the sweeping depression to where the smoke billowed. The hills had opened into flat country clumped with wattle and gum as hunting hides for the spearsmen but the hides had become overgrown through disuse as the spearsmen had been driven off. Later in the day they mounted a rise and Bill removed his hat and held it before the sun to shield his face as he studied the bivouac before them. Two white men wandered around the fire building it up. They had a captive bound and laid out in the grass. It seemed to be a naked black child. Bill replaced his hat and sat on the rocks and Katherine took seat alongside him and together they watched the goings-on. The men dragged the child around by the neck and dropped their pants and had turns with it. Bill looked away, then he looked back towards the men. He sat there awhile watching. A lone dog wandered near the fire. The child cried out.

It was enough. Bill picked up his gun and walked down the wooded hill. He meant to keep going, to make towards the coast where the Plindermairhemener were likely snugged up. He walked through the scrub and his ruined boots rang on the rocky ground. But Katherine did not follow. She remained staring out across the pasture. Bill waved to her but there was no response so he clambered back up to her lookout and stood beside her watching. She placed her hand inside his own and she pointed at the child. Pointed and squeezed his fingers. For a short time Bill stayed with her and clasped her calloused hand but then he rose and struck out for the camp.

...

They'd absconded from somewhere. That much was apparent from the broad arrows they still wore with their ankles and wrists exposed in those undersized government issues. One of them had a kangaroo skin cast about his shoulders like a cloak. His cohort carried a stout club. They waited by the fire as the Vandemonian crossed the field in full view. He cradled his piece in the bend of his arm and was some time reaching the place but he did not deviate nor did he move his eyes off the two men. As he neared, their dog started barking and its dorsal hair bristled.

She's trained to eat blacks that one, said the fellow in the skin cloak.

Black Bill walked unconcerned past the dog then stopped and glanced around their camp. A wallaby lay half in its entrails. Their hands were bloody and one of them had a knife. They stared at him.

I would use the fire if I might, said Bill.

You what?

The fire.

It talks, by Christ.

A talkin ape, aint it.

They both studied the long gun in Bill's arms.

I have a pipe. Some baccy. If you let me use your fire.

The one with the club leaned forward. What kinda darkie sports a gun like that? Eh?

Bill turned on his heel and began to walk back the way he had come but he hadn't gone more than a few steps when they called to him, Oi! Bring yer good self back here. We dont mean no harm.

He looked around at them. The dog snarled but stood off. He moved towards the fire again and took up a place in the grass. They'd humped up some firewood nearby for the night and propped against the heap was the native girl, no more than ten and collared with a length of roo hide. Bill kept his gaze away from her as he produced his pipe from his jacket, stuffed it with weed and passed it to one of the runaways. The fellow lit it with a handful of burning grass.

Holdin any rum about you there, blackie?

Bill shook his head.

No, I didnt reckon you was.

Why would some pisspoor old blackfella be holdin rum? said the other.

I supposed I might ask at least.

Did you now.

Who knows what he has stashed?

You howling bloody simpleton.

Their hair was matted like flocks of wool, their chins grimy with unshorn beards. They stared and he stared back.

Lookin to trade that piece are ye? said the man in skins.

Bill laid the weapon by but within reach. It was loaded, cocked. No, I have need of her, he said.

Take that dog for it. And some shot.

I dont need dogs.

Every bastard needs dogs.

Not every.

The man in skins stood up and moved around to Bill and held the pipe out and Bill accepted it with a nod, placed the stem to his lips and sucked. Flame leapt from the bowl as he puffed. He pushed back his hat. I wouldnt have thought females too common hereabouts, said Bill.

The men looked at each other and at the girl. She belong to you or somefink, blackie?

No.

The pipe hissed.

Got any kids have you then? said the man in skins.

I have a son.

Your kind ought to be gelded. You illbred fuckers.

The white men stared at him waiting for any signs of anger. But Bill just passed the pipe on and the man in skins closed his hand around the bowl, a hand shy its first and second fingers. His woody stumps tottered against the bowl as he drew. He watched Bill and Bill never blinked.

Is somethin painin you, blackie? he said.

I dont reckon.

Where'd you come from then?

Come out of them hills away west there.

The hills.

Aye.

Crept up liken old tomcat, didnt you?

The man in the skin cloak tapped out the spent pipe onto his palm. Make it the dog and the girl then, he said. And leave us a bit of ball.

No.

That's a fair offer.

No.

Out on the grass the emus raised their unclad heads, sounding their deep-throated drumming. The Vandemonian stood with his weapon, slung the strap over his shoulder and paused only a moment to stare at them, straightening his hat. He left for the hills and they watched him go. One of them called to him, You want yer pipe?

Bill never looked back. I'll find it after, he said.

They watched his dark figure shrink into the distance. The fellow in skins laid the pipe on the ground near the huge fire and looked at it. Then he turned his eyes back across the field where the Vandemonian retreated.

What's he mean, after? he said.

. . .

There was no moon at night so the scoundrels' fire shone upon the darkened plain like a sun alight in the universal vacuum. There was an hour or two before dawn and the men were curled in blankets soundly sleeping, the dog at their feet. By the fire the girl lay huddled, chewing at her bindings, working her wrists back and forth to loosen the cords and every so often she craned her head back to watch the slumbering men before she went again at the cords with her teeth. But the leathers in which she was cinched would not give and she could not advance her cause. Again she bent her head around to study the men where they slept, both with their mouths ajar and wheezing. When she turned back she saw something shifting beyond the light's throw. It seemed at first a trick of the mind or some other phantasm until she saw the steel blade in his teeth which showed him as separate from the night itself. The naked Vandemonian crawled nearer and cut her tethers.

laykara laykara. The words were thinly spoken.

But the girl only stared.

Bill pushed her. laykara.

Away into the dark the girl stumbled but her first movements woke the dog. It snapped up, baying as if for battle. The first of the men rose from his blankets and saw the severed ropes before the fire, saw the cleanly cut ends of them. As he surveyed the great unbroken blackness circling the camp he was caught from behind by the hair and a broad winking blade cleaved his throat to the vertebra. Holding the yawn in his flesh the fellow tumbled as blood burned down his arms and his heart pulsed everything onto the grass. The Vandemonian toppled him sideways onto the fire with one bare foot where his clothes burst alight and his rich blood bubbled in the depths of his wound.

The man in skins awoke to see the blazing body and even as he fumbled in his bedding the naked black man reared up from behind the fire pit, an archfiend smeared with gore. He leaned down out of the darkness but the man in skins scuttled out of his reach, found his feet and bolted into the undefined gloom. He ran blindly through the grass as the dog yowled somewhere behind him on the plain. Turning his head to sight his pursuer he saw the Vandemonian bearing down and made a sudden jag and changed flight. The naked black man was with him however and he threw himself forward and brought the coward down. They tussled on the ground. Bill rammed the knife into his back over and over again in cruel succession and the fellow screamed until his throat was opened upon the trodden grass.

Black Bill dragged the ruined corpse before the light of the fire where burned the first dead man and he stopped there to empty the fellow's pockets. A skinning knife spilled out, caked with fur, blunt, useless. Bill turned it in his fingers and threw it on the flames. The dog lay nearby watching him above its paws. Inside the fellow's waistband he found what he was searching for: his old oakwood pipe. He stuck the stem in his teeth, rolled the corpse squarely upon the coals and stood back as the skins blackened. With the bonfire at his back he set out across the grassland for the trees where Katherine was waiting and where he would sleep till dawn. The dog rose and began to trot behind him but he rounded on it and snarled through the darkness and the miserable thing cowered away, ears against its skull.

. . .

A thin watergrey autumn fog covered all the back country. On the broad and greasy gum leaves the dew beads balled and the sun showed only as a queasy presence pale beyond the gloom. It was under this muted dawn that Black Bill lay listening to the whistles of scrub wrens and honeyeaters, his hands stained with men's blood. He shook the dew off his possum skin and shouldered his fowling piece, looking for sign of his woman. He studied the range of dark mangy trees, looked along their length side to side, contemplating the trail he now saw Katherine had opened through the grass and the wet. After a minute he went onwards for the plain with an eye on the hills away east that were his landmark, hills that in the murk seemed mere rumour. As he walked he plucked a gum leaf and sat it on his lip.

He found her at the centre of a hunting ground, a broad span that she had bisected directly through the middle. Roos like a hundred gang men raised up their heads and studied the Vandemonian as he passed, but they did not flee, merely watching him while they chewed. Halfway across the open field he stopped. Katherine was crouched there collecting mushrooms and placing them in her shirt pockets. She looked up at him and handed over a fistful which Bill brushed off then placed into his mouth. They ate as they wandered through the mist, and the condensation formed on the loose strings of her hair and ran down her cheeks. Bill wiped her forehead and walked beside her.

. . .

The South Esk River ran through the farthest end of the valley. She was a long silverhaired old girl laid out in sand and stones and they were all the cold day reaching her. The river was edged with shrubs and leaning trees and they walked the bank a good while before finding a suitable place to cross at a little beach where the teacoloured water washed up in a lather of foam. They forded there in the shallows and upon the far shore Katherine was shuddering hard enough to crack her teeth. Bill watched her sitting purple with cold in the limeferns and he waited with her but she would not move. He knew they would go no further that day so he gathered the rudiments of a fire, struck a spark off his quartz into some wood fibres and in the withering light Katherine pressed in by the flames, outfitted in her blanket.

They had a nugget of possum meat in paperbark which Bill removed from his coat pocket and unwrapped. There wasn't more than a mouthful. He loosened his boots, unthreading the laces from the eyelets and knotting them together into a line. He tied on the possum meat and carried this crude tackle over to the water's edge barefoot. Billowed sails of final sunlight stood above the hills. He lobbed the meat beneath an overhang in the creek and sat there with the shadows filling around him. Sat there a good while until he felt the first tugs, then he drew the line inwards and teased the cray along. He put his face near the water and snatched at the creature, which flapped mightily, but he had it well caught. He scooped it onto the grassy bank.

The fire crackled. He stirred the embers with quick strikes of his hand, raised smoke and sparks, and he buried the crayfish in ash. Inside the coals the cray began to bubble at the mandibles and it clambered like a charred and smoking spider from the flames but Bill flicked it back into the coals where its legs soon curled inwards. He removed the cray and broke away the tail meat, which he passed to Katherine, keeping the head for himself. As he was fingering the yellow mustard from the carapace she clicked her tongue and tipped her head towards the river.

You see her? she said.

Bill dried his chin. I seen her.

She follow all day.

Yep.

Tell her go. We got no food. Got no blanket.

We have food now.

Katherine pulled white flesh from the tail. Tell her go.

luekerkener, Bill called out.

There was no reply.

tyerlarre luekerkener, he said again.

At first it seemed they were alone. Then the underscrub

along the river whispered as the native girl revealed herself. She was slight and her joints bulged through her skin; she watched the travellers out of eyes that knew hardship.

There now, he said. You tell her that yourself.

Katherine kept her face lowered, picking at the crayfish flesh, passing hunks of it up to her lips. On the river's far edge the girl stood waiting but Katherine would not look at her. The girl approached the stream and crossing the water she pulled herself onto the bank, huddling within her own arms as she came to crouch beside the fire. Bill gave the girl a few legs off the crayfish. Gave her his possum skin. The girl perched under the furs and cracked the shells apart and pulled the meat with her teeth. She wore no marks of initiation but what scars she had suggested kinship with coastal lands. Her bald head bore a stubble of regrowth. Bill watched her suck the meat from every stem and toss the shells on the coals. She licked her fingers clean.

How you feed her? said Katherine. How?

You wanted me to help her. Well I done that. Now she's on my ticket, aint she? I'll find her something, dont worry.

When they rolled up by the fire for sleep later on it was some time coming. The final violet sun had seeped away and the air began to grow ever colder as Bill loaded up the fire and lay back with his coat hunched around himself. Beyond the river the valley plain dimmed from view in the twilight. The girl watched the coals pulse but was silent. Bill propped himself nearer the flames and in the end he found some comfort backed against a river tree out of the wind and a fidgeting sleep overtook him in the small hours. Later he woke in the dark at some animal call and sat up and felt for his knife. The girl was staring into the fire as she had been, the milks of her eyes never moving. Bill studied that delicate face. He pulled his jacket up and shortly after drifted off.

. . .

Three wearied beings walked that humped land following a creeklet that vanished under rocks and hillocks. In the afternoon they broke off into the trees and at length crossed into a field of dunes where nothing grew save speargrass. The tops of dead trees showed clawlike in the sands, their trunks worn smooth. The travellers passed down the sand hills leaving divots where they stepped. They passed an escarpment of weathered stone and the Vandemonian kept his glance ahead but the girl arched her neck to see where the ridge met the living trees on the hill. Halfway along the length of the escarpment was a cleft run deep into the stone. The girl scrabbled down the dune and stood looking into the recess and then on her knees she stuck her head into the cave.

Bill saw that the girl was gone somewhere so he chose to have a spell in the shade and he eased down onto the stones and drank from the canteen, handing it to Katherine. The canteen passed between them as they waited. Shortly after the girl reappeared with something in her hands. As she approached they saw that it was a bullkelp waterbag. Bill thumbed back his hat. The waterbag was dried and stiffened and drawn closed with a braid of sinew. The girl squatted on the sands, placing the shapeless relic between them, but even before she'd buried her hand inside the pouch Bill was filled with the dire urge to stand and run. He got to his feet and when he looked at the girl she was extracting something darkly shrivelled from the bag. A slender desiccated hand, old beyond knowing. The girl turned it gingerly.

nara trew? she said.

In an instant Katherine stumbled away from the girl and her horrors, clambering up the dunes on all fours until, finding her feet, she made for the peak and Bill likewise bolted up the sands holding his hat as he ran. The two of them stood on the dune watching what the girl would do next and she seemed now to understand her error. She dropped the mummified hand and moved backwards. But as she shifted she upset the waterbag, spilling out a handful of leathered organs, a knot of black hair bound around in cord and a mess of painted votive stones. The girl stared at the grim remains.

You see now, said Katherine. That girl no good. I tell you this. She was squatting in the drifts and she dared not look at the girl or the grisly arrangement before her. No good, she said.

Bill waved his hand. Girl, come away from those things, he said. tyerlarre tyerlarre. They have power. They will hurt you. tabeltee.

The girl began to cry and she cried and would not stop. Katherine and Bill took up their burdens, walking on beyond the fringe of the little dune land and still the child cried and paced behind. They looked back at her but said nothing. Walking out of the dunes into the dry sedge and onwards into the gums, they left the relics cast upon the sands.

. . .

In a fathomless part of the night Katherine woke Bill and took his hand, leading him quietly away from the fire while the girl remained sleeping under her rug. She pulled him into the gum trees and further on into the scrub before she stopped.

She come?

No.

They crouched there a while listening to the flames snap through the tree limbs and thickets, listening for any sound from the girl. Nothing. Into the darkness they pushed, her hand in his, and they had gone some way when off in the scrub the girl was heard to cry out as she awoke alone. It was a sound alive with fear and Bill felt the pit of his gut twinge. He turned as Katherine came to a halt beside him and they crouched in the bush with that heartbreak ringing around them. Bill wiped the sleep from his eyes. He removed his hat and rubbed his hairless head. Then he rose and put back towards the campsite where it glowed in the distance. And Katherine followed him.

THEY TOILED FOR THE EAST THEREAFTER, the three of them, over the low hills, through the slackly grown coast scrub, then crossing plains still black where clans had burned back in passing. Two mornings out from the dune land they crested a rise and stretched out before them around the earth's curve was the eastern sea. They stood squinting into the shimmer as docile clouds amassed upon the misthazed horizon. Pushing through some tea-tree they came onto the sands where a wrack of bull kelp lay mangled along the tideline and the surf beat against the beach. With one hand shading his eyes Bill surveyed the shore and the assemblage of fur seals upon it. The seals rolled off into the waves in pairs and packs. He crouched, dug his fingers into the soft grains and rested there. After a time the girl found a stick and began digging a hole in the sand, reaching her arm into the wet below. Bill watched her work. Beach lice sprang up on the slag heap she'd made and she pulled up thready white worms and threw them into the water. Bill drove his arm down into the hole and heaved up a few handfuls too and the girl grinned. Together they dug deeper until sea water pooled in the hole and the sand ran as porridge. Katherine ignored them at their digging and walked off instead to gather mussels from the rocks. Along the beach the combers hit the shore, their spray curling and imploding.

As Bill lay on his stomach scratching in the sand he looked out across the sea. Skylit against the horizon was the grey shape of a gaff cutter nosing through the swell. He sat up. She worked a good way out but was bent tautly under her rigging and leaned into the wind as if she was well handled. He brushed the sand off his palms. No good size for whaling and more likely meant for putting about the shoreline after seals or swans or clanswomen. He caught the girl by the upper arm and hauled her into the trees where they might hide themselves.

He called to Katherine but she had seen it too. She tucked herself down behind the rocky headland and eyed the ship around the side. The cutter jounced across the whitecaps, making northerly at a clip, spray breaking on her bow. They remained hidden as she drew away. When she had receded Bill called Katherine closer.

We ought to go with her.

Eh?

Follow her north.

Follow?

Yes. A ship close in by the coast. Manalargena will find a means to get her trade. Be sure of it.

Katherine looked away. putiya, she said.

How else are we to find him? There is a lot of country out here and none of it friendly.

Them whites find us they take us.

I know it.

Take her, she said and indicated the girl.

Yes. Her especially.

No no no.

Then what? You mean to walk until your path crosses his?

She went down on her haunches. Took up a handful of sand and threw it.

In time Katherine stood up. She would not meet his eye but only dusted the sand from her palms and taking up her bundle walked along the beach, her feet in the dried sands squeaking like birds. So together they went along the shore with the cutter. Bill stayed off the beaches lest they were sighted by clansfolk and they tracked up and down the grassed sandbanks and through loose scrub stands. They crossed tidal creeks stained by the tea-tree and crowded with insect swimmers. Late in the day, as the sun burned into the hills, they looked up to see that the speck on the water had faded entirely from view. The sea was rolling inwards at their feet as they stood staring off to the north where the cutter had vanished beyond the boundaries of the world. There they stayed until

Bill called for a camp to be made and they dropped their heads and trudged into the scrub.

. . .

In the twilight they gathered driftwood and Bill knifed muttonfish from the stones below the tideline. They ate seaweed by the handful with the roasted muttonfish and drank Bill's canteen empty. As they ate, the girl and the woman stared at each other across the smoke. The girl was draped in the old worn rug that Bill had carried the length of the island. She turned away from Katherine and gave her attention to the coals instead.

After a while Katherine clicked her tongue at the girl. Eh, she said.

The girl looked up.

Katherine jabbed a finger at her. mullar walter nela?

The girl didn't answer.

She dont speak that tongue, said Bill.

Katherine looked at him.

Nor do I know hers worth a damn. I reckon she's come from further south. But how can I ask her?

Katherine tried again. wunnerrer noogee?

The girl seemed to consider the question as if it was something momentous. Her forehead rumpled up. She said, Moyhenna.

They could not be sure if she had understood.

In the firelight Katherine's face appeared to soften but it was only the light: behind it her features remained unmoved. She nodded.

They spoke no more after that. The cook fire died down as the sea winds played through the dunes, through the ratty wattles grown tip to tip and the florets of cutting grass. Bill leaned back, his eyes roaming the starlit sky. The stars themselves offered no counsel but he watched those teeming scintilla and marvelled at the promise their bright motes held.

. . .

They pushed up the coast two more days, eating well from the shoreline, sucking meat from seashells or yolk from swan eggs and taking weed off the rocks. When it rained they drank from rockpools and filled the canteen. On dusk they broke into the brittle coastal trees for a hidden place to sleep. Bill would not light fires now for smoke would show them up and in the morning they dragged branches through their campsite like outlaws and buried their waste in the sand. Surging waves crashed along the foreshore and the air was filled with a spray that sheared the sunlight into its constituent colours. They walked on around the bay's restless arc, their gangly morning shadows mocking them.

On the third day moving north they came upon a river

spilling onto a beach where terns rode the wind above the outpour and dived on the silver life they spied. Seals wallowed like monstrous infants in the wash, honking to each other over the roar of the waves. To the east the sun rose out of the sea and cast the headlands in a blue and formless gauze. Pods of whales blew water spouts in the bay, immense buds dispersing on the winds. But it was the ship that commanded their attention. Off in the bay's corner the cutter had heaved to and now bobbed dumbly on her anchor. The dinghy had been beached and hauled above the driftline, the oars left askew and sails lowered. At the distant end of the beach huge fires burned and the towers of smoke bent landward before the sea breeze.

Bill crouched long in the tea-trees surveying that scene, the cutter seesawing in the waves, her naked masts aloft. He watched the ship and at length he pulled the fowling piece off his back, removed the hood and charged a handful of ball down its belled throat. The girl knelt beside him and she ran her fingers over the hatching on the stock where the pattern had worn back but Bill pushed her roughly aside. When he was finished priming the gun he gave it to Katherine and stood behind a bush scanning each aspect of the camp along the beach. Then he removed his hat and knelt before the woman and the girl. The hat had lost its shape through hundreds of bush slogs and hung lifeless in his hands.

I see men moving around the fires, he said.

lamunika bungana?

Bill shook his head. Couldnt rightly say. But I reckon on him bein there somewhere.

Katherine stiffened. We go findim. Go now.

No. Not yet.

Why?

Let me think a minute. I need to think.

Bill pulled his hat brim through his fingers. He looked over his shoulder at the fires burning on the beach and he faced back to them and placed his hat upturned on the sand. Best wait for dark, he said.

Dark?

Yes.

Why wait for dark?

Same reason as any huntsman.

You no hide. Not from him.

Hiding aint my intention.

Manalargena bungana find you. He see you.

He will see what I'm about when I reveal myself. Not before.

Katherine flicked her hand, a dismissal.

You want to findim then go on. I wont stop you.

She peered into his eyes. You fear him.

Bill brought his knife out of its leathers, checked its blade and resheathed it behind his neck, turning again to study the fires burning in the far beyond.

There's no shame in saying it. That headman has no equal

in this life nor the next. But I know something else. No man can have his throat slit and still yap about it.

You cut him throat?

I will.

She held up the gun. Shoot him now. Walk there and shoot.

I tried that once. He never even fell. And him with that waddy of his, he near broke my head open.

How you get out?

Get where?

You cut him you run away?

Run like all buggery.

How?

I'll know a way when it presents.

They crouched there in the speargrass and sand dunes with the waves throwing a faint spray upon their skin. Watching the fires and the figures ambling around them. A cold wind angled in off the sea as the sun revolved behind a spread of cloud. They lay down out of sight and in that sheltered hollow they waited for nightfall.

ABOVE THE SALT MARSH THE MOON rose as white as parchment. The men of the Plindermairhemener, some Leetermairremener folk and some from even further south were gathered around the hearth fires by clan, a group convened from the remains of bands bitterly reduced by raids and wars and disease and every kind of misfortune the frontier could visit upon a people. The older men sat cross-legged near the fires on which crayfish shells steamed and oysters and mussels lined up on the stones had split open in the heat. They crunched meat and sand both and eyed the other clans eating likewise at their fires, whispering to each other. Naked, scarred and painted up like highlanders. They studied those foreign bands but if there were grievances and blood feuds unsettled they were set aside for the common cause of survival. For at the edge of the campsite, where the beach met the tussocked dunes, a party of whitefolk come in newly from the sea were stood around a great bonfire.

The seamen were of a sort common enough to those parts. They made a trade of skins and seal oil and they wintered in the islands of the strait where they had station camps arranged out of notice of the Royal Navy. At the fires they stood, sipping rum in tin mugs and taking chew dipped in the same, all outfitted in fur cloaks and breeches discoloured by the spilling of seal blood and shod in moccasins sewn from kangaroo tails. Beneath those vestments was hidden a selection of arms, leadweighted sealing clubs strung around their wrists, knives like bonesaws, and rusting pistols and hatchets meant for firewood. They spat tobacco liquor on the flames and crimped the fleas picked from their beards between the nails of thumb and forefinger. The whites did not come alone. Crouched among them were half a dozen black women taken or traded over the years from the coastal tribes. These native wives filled the men's mugs from a communal bucket and roasted their potatoes in the coals, and while the wives worked they sang of the Christian devils who were their keepers. A doleful tune that sounded in essence like tribal chanting but bore the melodic rise and fall of a ballad. The seamen drank down their rum and stared at the young clan girls seated at the hearth fires with the natives and these girls lowered their eyes or looked away. But their meekness would not save them.

So when the Vandemonian appeared among the fullest shadows of the fire's peripheries, a lone figure come on a sudden from the sedge lands beyond, the wives sang and the seamen drank and for a time he remained anonymous. In the dark he searched around those faces for the headman, each face more grim than the one before. As he looked across the camp he saw one of the whites leave off from drinking and wander towards him through the shrubs and he felt for his knife. The seaman had a pannikin in hand and he sidled up to Bill, swaying beside him in the dimness as he raised the mug to his mouth with a staggered precision. He bore the flag of Nantucket stitched onto his lapel, the whale and the circle, and in his beard was a long beaded braid much in the manner of the old Norsemen. Rum drizzled down his chin into his whiskers. His earlobes were stretched like teats under a weight of iron hoops and he was pierced through the nose and lip as well. The fellow scratched himself.

Where'd you all come from? he said.

The Vandemonian looked at him, then looked away.

Kit up like all whatever. You dont look like no coon in that hat. The American swayed and shifted his feet to right himself. A bit of rum sloshed from his mug. I knowed a lot a coons too.

The wives struck up a new song that sounded like some sort of shanty and the seamen added their voices to it and sang with an affinity and feeling to which the elders at the hearth fires listened politely but did not understand.

Are you one of these yahoos?

Black Bill spat to one side.

Damn sure dont look like em.

A veteran, unusually stout through the forearms, started stepping out an impromptu jig. This spectacle raised a round of catcalls from the gallery as the shambling man went about on the sands holding up his thick arms like the wings of a grounded carrion bird and the clansmen seated at their family fires laughed openly at the foolishness.

The American gestured at Bill with his mug. You dont understand a word I'm speakin do ye? You half-assed nigger.

But as he turned to stagger off, a tall, broadchested figure came trotting through the campsite with children clinging to his legs. In the middle of that eccentric muster the children of the clans had begun upon a game and they stalked this big fellow through the camp's darkened borders. Children squealed in delight and swung off his legs to bring him down but the fellow howled in their ears and freed them to begin the chase again. That reckless pack harried him between the trees, dogs and children both, the dour lumbering demon fleeing in feigned terror. Through the dust of the jig, the smoke and stink, the Vandemonian saw him, unsheathed his dagger and established a stance with his blade shining and his bleak purpose reflected in his features.

bungana, he called.

The game suddenly ended. With the children still ranked up around his legs Manalargena turned to regard the Vandemonian. The headman was breathing heavily, sweating. The men around the fires numbered perhaps twenty and they rose on his word. The clatter of clubs and spears being taken up killed off the singing. The seamen also fell silent and some backed slowly into the darkness out of sight while some brave souls felt for their weapons.

So he come, said the headman. The cold wind. The cold wind. In he blows.

By God you put that down. The American had pulled an archaic duelling pistol from the rope in his pants and steadied it at Bill's temple. Put it down and stick up yer hands.

Bill did not move. He watched the headman.

Stick em up less you want yer whole upper storey blowed off, you son of a bitch.

He no listen. No hear. The headman shook his head.

He'll damn well hear me soon he doesnt drop that blade.

Put away gun, said Manalargena.

I said drop it.

When Bill moved the knife came so fast and precise that the American never even gasped until Bill was upon him. He grabbed the pistol, pushed it aside and as it fired into the sand he cut the muscle of the man's upper arm with a single pass. The American hollered and clamped his hand on the wound. He stumbled back towards his crewmates. They looked at each other nervously, gaffs and knives and oars held up in defence. Once at the fire the American dared to lift his clamped hand to study the laceration but the sight of his arm laid bare caused him to wail and fall to the sand.

The headman never removed his eyes from Bill. orrercarner nicker?

I mean to take my redress.

Manalargena came forward and the children arranged around his legs moved with him. He rested his empty hands on them, stroked the head of a spindly girl. And my daughter? You kill her? My sister son? He touched the children in turn as if to indicate them.

I do what needs doing.

You keep sorrow, said the headman. He touched his cheeks. Keep it here. But sorrow is you deserve. It is belong to you.

His men, all armed for warring, ranged out behind their leader now in a crude division. Among that mix of clansmen all knew the deeds of Bill's history and they knew the havoc he'd sown in their lands as a vassal of Batman. When Bill inched forward with his knife displayed the warriors were stayed by his fearful standing and they raised no cries of war nor called on their ancestors but heard only the squeal of his boots through the sands. He moved and his blade glimmered.

I speak truth here, said Manalargena. You strong man. Yes. But you cannot eat stone. Not stone.

Manalargena reached down to pick up a hand axe off the rocks. It was a simple tool meant for dressing animals and a mess of fur remained around the heel from this work. Its iron head was hafted on a hardwood waddy and affixed in place with resin. It bore no adornments of any kind save for ridges along the handle and the blade was notched where it had struck against bone or rock. He held this curious weapon down by his side. On the beach the fires twisted.

You did something to my boy. I know it.

Ah. The child.

What did you do?

Yes. The child is justice. Your owing is paid.

Without any sort of notice Bill lunged forward and swung the knife at the headman's gut then slashed it upwards. The startled children fell away behind the ranks of men. Manalargena skipped back, clutching the hand axe to his chest.

The child was no part of this, said Bill.

He moved in again and whipped the knife left and right in a motion as fast as a snake strike and this time it caught the headman across the wrist and opened a wound. The clansmen stationed at his back lifted their spears and beat their waddies on the shafts and the clamour grew as they readied to attack.

The headman stuck out his axe. mullarner! he said.

They halted. Some made war calls and others leered at him but they did not ship their spears. A flow of blood began down the headman's fingers and he flicked it away. He continued pacing and watching the Vandemonian where he stood with his knife at his waist.

I not kill you, Tummer-ti. This is finish. You go now. As he pointed out across the marsh tussocks blood ran from his

270

fingers, ran down the thousand scars crisscrossing the skin of his blighted arm.

He was my son.

Bill swung his knife again. The blade passed cleanly by the headman's throat and before that movement ended he'd caught Bill's arm and turned it against his shoulder. Bill was pushed off balance. In a stroke the headman brought around his axe and buried it to the marrow in Bill's thigh. The Vandemonian cried out. The headman jerked the edge free and a flow of blood splashed down Bill's leg. They backed away and stood facing across that small distance, the headman bearing his axe like a butcher's hatchet and the sand beneath Bill's feet thickening with his blood. His leg, his whole side, was in torment.

Go, said the headman. Again he pointed into the darkness.

Bill spat, his eyes like gun black.

Manalargena brought up his arms. His gaze swept across the clansfolk. nara relipianna clueterpercare, he said.

This was met with the crackle of waddy on spear.

Then Manalargena looked to the American. He brave man, yes?

Son of a bitch near cut off my arm. He needs hacking up is what he needs.

Once more Manalargena faced the Vandemonian, waving his axe around in agitation. You murder us. You come in the night. You hide. You shoot. With pimdimmeyou you come. And you bring sorrow. So I call your child and he listen. My demon call. He hear our music that child. This is justice, he said.

Blood pooled in his boot. His hand was weak around the dagger and he focused on sounds nearby as he tried to slow his labouring heart and fight the nausea brewing in his gut but there was so much pain he could think of nothing else. After some breaths he raised his eyes to the unbending frame of the headman. He clutched his knife and limped forward.

Come, said the headman, and I teach you.

Bill aimed for the ribs, came up and under. The headman knocked his arm wide and brought around the blunt side of his axe to crack Bill on the nape. It was a heavy blow and he staggered. Now the headman caught his knife arm and he fought Bill backwards onto the sand where he straddled his chest and angled the axe hilt across Bill's throat. Bill struggled and kicked but the headman leaned his weight upon the handle and pushed to stop the air in his neck. Bill's knife arm was pinned to the sand. His vision began to flicker. Seamen jeered and whistled. Then the headman eased off.

This is finish. You go. Go now.

Manalargena stood up and paced back out of reach. The Vandemonian gasped air as he rolled onto his side. The wild men ringing around him with spears and waddies and seal clubs called on him to stand and fight. He raised himself to his knees. But even as he felt for his knife in the sand a shot boomed out on the salt marsh. The headman slumped. Fiery red stipples appeared along his leg where buckshot had entered the flesh and he pressed his hands to the holes and blood seeped through his fingers bright against the dark of his skin.

Now a general confusion seized hold of the camp. Some of the clansfolk picked up the headman and carried him into the firelight and others scattered away in fear of being shot but one or two looked at the Vandemonian and they raised their waddies to beat him where he crouched. He drew his body into a huddle but the blows against his ribs were skilfully delivered and drove the wind from his lungs.

noneta! noneta! noneta!

A woman's voice cleaved the discord of the campsite. In that moment the waddy blows ceased and the clansmen ran. Bill scrabbled away over the sand holding his damaged leg and when he raised his eyes he saw Katherine revealed from the darkness by the fire's irregular glow, and borne at her hip was his fowling piece. She approached and those clansmen fled like children before the muzzle of her gun. But her intentions lay not with them at all and when one of their number pitched a spear she knocked it aside with the barrel and then renewed her levelled gaze upon the headman.

He was lying near the fires. His wounds and his bloody fingers were grimed with sand and he wore a look of great astonishment at the sight of her. The clansfolk around him had bolted into the night. Down on the beach the sealers were mounting their masted dinghy into the breakers and their calls for haste could be plainly heard above the waves. Only the seamen's wives remained and as Katherine stalked into the campsite they began upon a song. It was a canticle of the devil's prowess in war and the soothing words he spoke for the dying as he dispatched them towards his own realm on the point of his waddy. From the beach the whites called to their wives but the women sang on and on.

Manalargena faced her across the smoke and flame. The mother, he said. Yes. Shoot, Mother, or go. I not fear you.

She thumbed back the mechanism.

Bill rose off the sands, bloodstained and beaten. Leave him be, he said. Leave him.

He placed his hand on the barrel and tried to push it down. She shoved him off but he gripped the piece and would not let go.

There is nothing here, he said.

In the dark of the dunes the clansfolk gathered together and they enjoined the headman to flee but he paid them no attention. He sat staring into the great black cavern of the muzzle. pressing his hands to the pits driven into his leg. Sand and blood in his wounds mixed in rich amalgam. Then Katherine screamed at him. A long torn miserable wail ripped from the very well of her being. In the face of it the headman merely raised one hand to her, showing blood and sand both.

Bill hauled at her elbow and called on her to move. She lowered the gun. Shouldered it. The wives sang on yet she would neither look at them nor would she listen. The two together left the camp and no one dared follow.

So it passed that none of them noticed the girl. The remnant clans reconvened at dawn in the long golden sun blades angling over the water. On the bluestone sea the gaff cutter leaned under her sails and as she hauled away, the clanspeople stood along the shoreline, their faces impassive. Manalargena was consulting with his demon silently before the fire. He had removed the shot balls by means of a glass spear point, washed his wounds in the sea and dressed them with pounded herbs, and now he allowed the leg to dry in the fresh air. His eyes were closed and as he whispered his scarred arm twitched with life. When it was done he led his people down the coast, the women and children from the south and east, the men of his own clan. As that conglomerate people walked the girl tracked along behind them over the coastal plains, keeping them in sight as she made through the tea-trees and candle heath ranged above the beaches. She clasped a possum skin around her shoulders and in her hands a bundle of shellfish rolled in soft bark and knotted. Things given to her by Black Bill and his woman. On dark the remnant tribe settled in around a cook fire and the girl watched them for a time from her hide and then she descended out of the grassed dunes and into their campsite.

THEY WALKED THROUGH THE DARK HOURS, the Vandemonian limping badly, and in the early pallid dawn they saw from a balded peak the sea laid out like slate miles to the east. The waxing sun lit the speargrass marsh but there was no sign of men crossing that range in pursuit. They rested for a time as Bill vomited quietly over the stones and paraffin bush and dried his forehead on his sleeve each time after the pain swept his body. Katherine led him through the gums at a slow pace, with Bill holding onto every trunk and overhang and favouring his good leg. Blood had congealed inside his boot and each step sounded an odd swampy suck from its depths. They pushed on down a shaded ridge where the branches curled under a weight of glossy herbage and it brushed against them without cease. In that shade the cold was compounded as their clothes took the dew from the leaves. Bill shivered and hopped down the embankment until he could go no further and he called to Katherine. At first she kept on walking for a dozen yards or so, with no sign it seemed of any kind of mercy. He slumped down at the base of a blackwood and stretched his ruined leg out in front of him. He could not see her and he waited in silence before she reappeared.

She came up the slope and stood assessing him at a distance, her few provisions bundled with the fowler on her back, her blankets horseshoed across one shoulder, a sort of sullenness on her face which he knew as its chief feature. He waved her closer. Silvereyes were roosted there in profusion and as she approached between the trees they took up in warning to each other. She leaned over Bill and gripped hold of his thigh to better know the injury, turning it this way and that until he gritted his teeth all the harder for the pain. Straightening up she began to unload her blankets and bits and pieces onto the ground beside him and she walked out among the pine and white gum and currant bush mounted on that shadowed ridge and went from tree to tree gazing up into the highest parts, her great double braid of black hair trailing like a mooring rope down her back. She selected one tree which appeared most likely and all the while the little silvereyes warbled. From out of the rubble, the blown branches and bark and leaves, she picked up a chunky stick and walked back to Bill. He hoisted himself upright with it and followed her through the shrub to the blue gum she had chosen. She hooked her foot into his hands and clambered onto the bottom limb where she found some holds that allowed her to ascend the trunk at speed. Bill watched her vanish into the canopy. He sat down and waited.

In the end he heard the possum long before he saw it. The silvereyes had fallen silent and Bill was lying back as if he might fight off the pain through sheer force of will. He heard the catsounding screams and looked up but could see nothing of Katherine through the tangle. He watched and waited and soon a shape came tumbling out of the tree limbs and thudded in a rise of dust upon the stones. Bill was over it, hobbling, clubbing it around the head, and the possum gave one short smothered yowl as it made to flee but Bill brained the thing mightily. He took it up by its curled tail and turned it in the sunlight, knocking aside the joeys clinging precariously to the pouch, and carried the carcass to a clearing where a fire could be stacked. Katherine came backwards down the trunk and hung off the final branch, swinging to and fro then dropping to her feet.

They roasted the possum below the shade of the sassafras and ate every part, ate the tail and the eyes from its skull—one each—and fried the giblets on a skewer. When they were done Katherine chose the thinnest of the forearm bones and with the knife she halved it down the centre, then quartered it. She took up one quarter and worked the tip into a point by filing it against a stone. Bill was stretched out near the fire and in the measured light his face was grey and his eyes mooned oversized in their sockets. He watched her stand and strip off her pants and using the bone needle she proceeded to pick loose a few threads of cotton which unwound like tiny worms into her sandcoloured palm. Greasing the thread with a dab of possum fat she passed it

279

through the eyehole she'd cut into the bone. Then she shuffled over to Bill. He rolled onto his side to present to her the cleft hacked in his thigh. From the ground he retrieved a stoutlooking piece of black gum and placed it between his jaws.

Every pass was purest distress. Katherine gathered the livid flesh together in a pucker and pressed the needle through and her hands were heavy with blood, and blood and sweat ran in equal proportion through Bill's clothes and dampened the litter beneath. He did not cry out but bit down on the wood until his lips also bled. Finally it was at an end. She tied the thread, bit it off, and towelled her hands on her pants before she pulled them on again. Bill lay on his pallet of twigs and leaves, his eyes half closed, palms open, and he did not see her take the knife and put out into the trees.

When he awoke it was near on dark. He had a great thirst and he sat up and cast about for the canteen. Katherine was staring at him across the fire and she tossed the bottle through the smoke and onto his lap. He winced as it struck. His thigh was bound up in a poultice of tea-tree leaves and the vapours they shed brought water to his eyes. A wrap of paperbark fixed the poultice in place, the whole like some tumorous growth of his own flesh, seeping greenish ooze. He drank deeply and slumped back.

Why him not kill you? she said.

Bill opened his eyes. What?

Why him not kill you?

He looked at her. He shook his head.

Old now that bungana. Old. Dumb. I would kill you.

Yes. I reckon you would.

He closed his eyes and lay still in the fire's warmth. A wind rolled in that stirred and reddened the coals. Bill screwed up his eyes for the smoke drifting past. He lay back alone with the misery in his leg.

Manalargena told me a story once, he said. My father used to sing the same story whenever we saw a snake. He'd point to the snake and start up singing but Manalargena's story differed on some points. His folk have their own telling I reckon.

Story, she said. She stoked the fire with a possum bone. What story?

It concerns these two brothers, said Bill. And their neighbour.

He was quiet for a spell. Then he said, I hear you now.

After a while Katherine rose and stepped past the fire and handed him the tiny skull she wore always at her throat. Mooncoloured and frail and jawless. Bill cupped it in his palm, this last piece of a son he'd known only in dream. He looked upon that relic, desolate of heart as he spoke the boy's name, the secret name he had given, and he said goodbye in his old tongue. He caressed that pearled bone and he promised the boy he would not forget him. He lay there for a long time with wind dousing his skin, watching a cinder sky churn above the forest, the skull clutched in his hands and his son's secret name upon his lips. Longing for the deep dreams when he would visit.